WICKED CITY

WICKED CITY books by Hideyuki Kikuchi

Wicked City: Black Guard

Look for Wicked City: Book 2 coming 2010!

WICKED CITY BLACK GUARD

HIDEYUKI KIKUCHI

TOR®

Seven Seas

A TOM DOHERTY ASSOCIATES BOOK
NEW YORK

WICKED CITY: BLACK GUARD

Originally published as *Youjyu Toshi* by Shodensha in Tokyo, Japan. Copyright © 1985 by Hideyuki Kikuchi.

Tor / Seven Seas edition copyright © 2009

All rights reserved. English translation rights throughout the world arranged with Shodensha through Tuttle-Mori Agency, Inc., Tokyo.

English translation by Ben Wood

English adaptation by Christine Norris

Interior illustrations by Jennyson Rosero

A Tor/Seven Seas Paperback
Published by Tom Doherty Associates, LLC
175 Fifth Avenue
New York, NY 10010

Seven Seas and the Seven Seas logo are trademarks of Seven Seas Entertainment, LLC. Tor® and the Tor logo are registered trademarks of Tom Doherty Associates, LLC.

Visit us online at www.gomanga.com and www.tor-forge.com.

Book design by Greg Collins

ISBN 978-0-7653-2330-9

First U.S. Edition: October 2009

Printed in the United States of America

0   9   8   7   6   5   4   3   2   1

CONTENTS

BLACK GUARD

PART ONE

1

IT WAS one of those rare days when I actually finished all my work on time. I left the office with every intention of heading straight home. But as soon as I climbed out of the subway car in Shibuya, I realized that wasn't going to happen. I drifted through the station, another drop in a sweltering ocean of liquid bodies, and spilled out of the Hachiko exit.

I crossed the intersection, and headed up Hyakendana. I soon arrived at my seedy destination. A neon sign flickered overhead—*Vesuvius*—enticing me, drawing me in like a bee to a nectar-laden flower.

The joint was already more than eighty percent full. I was

greeted by the mellow rhythms of soft rock mingled with a few warm welcomes. Vesuvius was a simple chug and tug. It had a reputation among those in the know for great service and cheap prices. The drinks weren't all that bad either.

"Taki! I thought you'd forgotten about us!"

I gently unpried the white arms wrapped around me and asked the girl attached to them if Belle was working tonight.

"Oh, not her again?" she said with what was supposed to be an adorable pout. "Don't you want a little something different tonight, Taki-baby?"

Another girl chimed in with her two cents. "Yeah, how'd you get to be such a company hotshot when you're so damn predictable?"

Even as they yammered on, they scanned the place, looking for my girl.

A third girl, whose name also escaped me, put a hand on the mouth-watering curve of her hip. "Strange. I know she's here somewhere. No one else requested her tonight, so maybe she's still fixing herself up."

"Evening, Taki." Another one of the girls drifted past in a haze of perfume. "Looking for little Belle, are we? I saw her heading to the changing room earlier with Leona."

The first clingy girl pointed to someone coming toward us. "Well, speak of the devil . . ."

Through an intoxicating cloud of purple smoke, cheap booze, and murmuring voices, a stunning beauty emerged, clad in a mini-skirt that left nothing to chance. I'd never seen her before . . . which meant she must be Leona.

Our eyes met and her lips twitched upward, nervously. She gave a slight, awkward bow. Her smile was stiff, forced. *A naïve one, eh?*

One of the girls introduced us. "Taki here is but a sad little businessman who slogs through his working day just to catch a glimpse of Belle's pretty face. Look at him, pale with fright, panicked that some other guy has stolen his girlfriend away." The girls laughed, at my expense.

Leona bowed again, just as irresistibly as before. "A pleasure to meet you. I'm Leona." She looked up at me shyly, through long, delicate lashes. "Belle left ahead of me. I'm surprised you missed her. I'll go find her for you."

"Hold on, that's okay. I'll take you instead. I feel like a change tonight after all."

The first girl feigned shock. "You big cheat!"

Another cocked her head sideways. "Now this is exactly why you should never get married!"

As they teased on, I nodded to a waiting male staff member. He led me into one of the small back rooms.

My reason for visiting a place like this? Maybe since it was on my way home and relatively safe and easy. Or maybe it was just plain and simple force of habit. Or maybe . . . I don't care to ponder the reason. Whatever the excuse, the reason I always asked for Belle was out of sheer laziness. I didn't want to expend the energy trying to find new talent. But that changed with one glance at Leona. I was ready for something different. She had none of the smooth, practiced manner of the other girls. Her hesitant demeanor and girlish embarrassment didn't appear to be forced. Coupled

with the sheer purity I saw in her face, I was well on my way to ecstasy in less than ten minutes.

In another twenty, thirty minutes I'd be ready for Round Two. As I rattled on about my sales record of the past month, Leona suddenly looked into my eyes and blurted out, "You're a little old for me, but I think I'm gonna like you. You're sweet, you know that? You're not into any of that weird stuff."

"A little old for you? Please, I'm only twenty-five." Playing hurt wasn't really my style, but it seemed to work wonders.

"Taki, can I ask you a question? When I get off work, would you like to come back to my place?"

"Excuse me?" Even I couldn't keep my cool in the face of this sudden development. Leona muttered, "Oh, I've done it again," and looked up at me, pressing her hand to her cheek. Even in the inky dimness of the small room, the flushed crimson of her face was clearly visible. Now, this was sheer ecstasy.

Leona said she would get off work early. I left Vesuvius ahead of her, killing time for thirty minutes or so before heading to the café where we'd arranged to meet. Right on time, there she was, smiling, happy to see me. I started to go inside, but she signaled for me to stay where I was and bounced joyfully into my arms.

We chatted as we walked to the taxi stand. It turned out Leona was a college student, living in a cheap one-room-plus-amenities apartment between Shibuya and Harajuku. She had started working at Vesuvius four days ago and be-

came especially close to Belle in that short time. I asked if Belle had shown up after I left, but Leona remarked how strange it was, that Belle had just disappeared, and all the girls were starting to get worried. The last thing Leona remembered was being with Belle in the changing room and then watching her leave suddenly.

I tried to console her. "Don't you worry, I'm sure she'll turn up sooner or later."

"I know." Leona nodded, reassured. "How about we talk about something else, okay? Tell me everything about you."

I shrugged. "Nothing much to tell, really. Name's Renzaburo Taki, twenty-five years old. I'm 180cm, 65 kilos, blood type AB. I work for a central electronics company in Ginza. Monthly income: 230,000 yen, after taxes, plus bonuses twice a year. No wife, no kids. I live alone in a two bedroom apartment in the Suginami ward of Hamadayama."

A taxi arrived by the time I finished. When Leona heard those last details of my life, she clapped her hands together. "Then I'm in luck! But still . . ."

"Still, what?"

"I don't know. I can't help feeling there's more to you than meets the eye."

"What makes you say that?"

Leona shook her head. "I'm not sure. It's just a feeling I have about you. Like you're different somehow. You really just work for some electronics place?"

"Of course. I've got my ID right here if you don't believe me."

"Hmmmm." She left it at that . . . or rather, didn't have time to say anything else. She suddenly told the driver to stop, and the two of us climbed out into the steamy night.

Leona's apartment building was nearer to Harajuku than Shibuya. White-walled but a little too close to the invasive rumble of the Yamanote train line, it was big and bare. There was no one in the lobby other than the two of us.

Leona's room was on the seventh floor. She might have described it as a one room apartment with modest facilities, but I felt lost standing in the middle of the expansive space almost fifteen tatami mats in size. My own place, for all of its two rooms, could barely scrape together seven tatami. Mine was made of simple mortar; hers reinforced concrete.

"You keep the place pretty tidy, don't you," I said, impressed.

"Why do you sound so surprised?" Leona's voice drifted faintly from the kitchen, where she was preparing drinks.

"No, it's just that, back in my college days I saw my fair share of girls' rooms. Girls love, you know, girly stuff. Cuddly toys and piles of clothes and all sorts of clutter all over the place. I practically had to trample my way over their junk. But you don't have a thing to your name."

"I straightened up the other day." Leona emerged from the kitchen and placed a tray with a frosty pitcher of beer and a smaller glass onto the carpet. In a fine impression of a quick change artist, she had changed out of her work clothes and into a long, flared skirt and a simple woolen sweater.

I glanced behind her. "Wouldn't it be better to drink at the table in the kitchen?"

"That's hardly homey. I have a better idea. I'll run a bath for you."

"Hey, hold it. You're a single girl, living alone. I can hardly take advantage of you like that."

Leona's smile was catlike and she practically purred. "Don't worry. We're not taking it together." With a sly wink, she stood and headed for the bathroom. After a few moments she was back, dropping down close to me. She poured beer, her hands now moving with a relaxed confidence. Perhaps having left work and back now in familiar surroundings, she was starting to show her true colors. Women can be devils like that.

She seemed happy enough to just sit there and watch me down a few beers. Before long, she took a long, slow swig herself and moved her glistening lips towards mine. I did not resist.

As she pressed her soft, moist lips against mine, the sensation of cool liquid commingled with Leona's warm tongue in my mouth. Her right hand moved to my thigh, and like a second tongue, flickered toward my crotch. She moved with a hungry grace, in desperate need of fulfillment. The vigor of her tongue exploring my mouth, pushing behind my gums, and the eagerness of her hand stroking the growing bulge in my trousers hardly jibed with her earlier reserve.

With her free hand she grabbed my right and guided it toward her own most intimate region. She wasn't wearing the eye-popping mini skirt from work, but my hand soon found the hot, damp place between the tops of her thighs.

"You know, maybe I'll join you after all . . . in the bath." She was standing even before she finished murmuring into my ear. She walked around me and drew aside the accordion-style partition that divided the bathroom area from the rest of the apartment and slipped inside. Alone for a moment, I glanced around the spotlessly clean, almost unlived-in room, and wondered why, exactly, she had invited me here.

Her honeyed voice drifted from behind the partition. "Don't keep me waiting." Suddenly she was behind me. She coiled her arms around me and loosened my tie. Her fingers moved across the buttons of my dress shirt and began to dance on the bare skin of my chest.

"Oh, how lovely you are. So manly." Her voice, heavy with desire, had lost the last remnant of the innocence that she had displayed back at Vesuvius.

What else could I do? I stood, facing her, and was greeted by a bust far fuller than I had guessed. Plenty more thigh was also on display, barely concealed by a light green bath towel. The quivering pinkness of her skin was a tantalizing sign of things to come.

She handed me a towel that matched the one she wore.

"Here, take this. I've already taken a shower." She headed back to the bathroom, leaving me with a light, burning kiss before she went. I headed after her, slipping out of my clothes and putting the towel around my waist.

In the bathroom, Leona still wore her towel.

She gently blocked my outstretched hand with two fingers. "Not yet. I want to do something nice for you first." She crouched in front of me and unraveled the towel from my waist. She gazed upon my exposed manhood and grinned. "Oh, aren't you a cute little thing? I wonder how you taste."

Without hesitation, her head darted forward, and her lovely red lips took me between them. An amazing sensation rippled up my spine as I closed my eyes in rapture, losing sight of the seductive expression on Leona's face as she serviced me. She intensified the feeling of her tongue on the head of my cock, almost as if countless tongues were sliding over my glans.

Purring in the back of her throat like a cat, she reached around my buttocks with her right hand and started to finger my asshole. I grew harder by the second, expanding to fill her luscious mouth. Just as I was about to shoot my load, she stopped and stood. She whispered in my ear. "I want you to stick it in me right now."

"Lose your towel, then."

"I will when you're inside me. My tits are so big and soft. Don't worry, you're in for a surprise."

"I'll bet." I pushed Leona against the wall and pulled

up her left leg. My other hand gripped her curvy waist. Exposed to the steam and lights, her vagina remained an innocent pink. But her thoughts were not.

"Do me now. Fuck me hard."

In response to her sultry command, I thrust into her, pushing between the hot, soft layers of flesh. With each shove of my hips, the sensation of her sticky juices and the tightness of her pussy generated the kind of pleasure that would have caused most men to spill themselves in five or six thrusts.

"Oh, I like you. So big and strong." Even as she urged me to thrust harder, she placed a hand to her towel.

"There's something you should know . . ."

"Huh?"

"I told you before I didn't know where Belle was . . ."

"Right?"

"Actually, I do. You see, I was just so fond of her. She was so sweet to me, inviting me to dinner and all."

"So?"

"I wanted to be with her. Never apart. So, just before you came in, we were in the back together . . ."

Her white hand removed the towel. "And I did this."

Her hips stopped thrusting, and I got a complete view of her naked torso. I wish I hadn't. Something bulged, like the back of a whale, from beneath her skin. It ran all the way from her navel to just under her voluminous tits. A pair of eyes, glimmering with the pain of endless suffering and depthless hatred, glared at me from inside the blue-black lump. Beneath the eyes was a straight nose and a mouth that opened and closed like some desperate diver on the verge of drowning. It was Belle's face, twisted in indescribable pain, frozen in a visage of empty horror beyond death.

Leona, face still so close to mine, laughed. "What do you think?" She smiled and her mouth unfurled like a flower of torture. Pure white teeth, inhuman in shape, jutted from between her wide, red lips. The whites of her eyes, wide-open, gradually changed to an unearthly purple.

I tried to shove her off me, but my arms stuck to her skin as though she were coated with glue. A second later I realized I had actually pushed my hands into her body. Suddenly there was a strange feeling in my head, as though something was sliding across my brain and into my thoughts. Was it pain? Even though it felt as though both of my hands were melting away, my lower organ, still inside Leona, remained in a state of indescribable ecstasy. The warm, moist flesh of her pussy turned into countless tongues, licking at my member and leading me, impossibly, toward a peak of inhuman pleasure. Even as my lower body trembled in pleasure, my upper body screamed out in pain.

"That's good, baby, very good," Leona said, breathily. Her seduction remained unchanged, though her face was now a parody of her former innocence. "It's been over one hundred years since I had a human male. Does it hurt, poor baby? I suggest you sit back and enjoy the experience. You know, I think I've fallen for you. I'm going to become one with you too, just like Belle."

WICKED CITY · BLACK GUARD

Even as she finished speaking, my arms sunk further into her body, elbow-deep. Her breasts melted into my chest, and her slimy stomach began fusing with my abdomen. It occurred to me that anything absorbed by Leona would go on to receive nutrition from her for the rest of her life, enduring both endless pain and pleasure, like Belle, neither truly alive nor truly dead. But for how long? Just how long would Leona live, anyway?

Her mouth, shaped like a crescent moon, closed in on mine. Those adorable lips that had poured beer into my mouth kissed me again. This time our mouths fused together as though melted by fire, followed by our teeth. Yet her tongue continued to stroke my own, as though offering condolences for this terrible transmutation of my existence. Leona spoke into our fused mouths.

"Hurry up and finish, baby. Cum inside me before you die. Semen is what gives us such long life." Her vagina stroked my member, and even as the burning desire to ejaculate pressed down upon me, I resisted the urge. I jerked away from her body and her face changed, giving me a glimpse of the monster she truly was.

And that's when she realized who she had gotten mixed up with. "You . . . you're not . . . !" Her cry inside my mouth was cut short by the sound of flesh being torn asunder. Something raw and warm flopped into the cavern formed by our joined mouths. I pulled my head back as hard as I could. I'd ripped Leona's teeth away, gums and all, drenching my face and throat in purple blood.

Blood from another world poured like a waterfall on the towel that lay on the floor.

With that terrible second set of eyes still watching, eyes loaded with unspeakable pain and shock and rage, I tore our bodies apart. Flesh was ripped from Leona's abdomen, and her internal organs spilled out with a soft, wet, splash. Finally, I yanked my arms free, with no regard for the flesh around them. As I tore two more holes in Leona's body, the rest of my naked body came free along with chunks of meat in my hands and the entrails of my assailant.

"That'll teach you to hit on a Black Guard," I said quietly. "But why attack me now? We still have some time before the Treaty expires." I waited for an answer, but none came. I picked up the wriggling sliver of flesh that had been Leona's tongue from the floor and regarded it. "I guess you can't answer me now, can you?"

Her jaw missing, with massive holes ripped in her thighs, arms, and stomach, the once beautiful woman now slumped to the floor, body ruined, covered in a pool of purplish blood.

"You may be able to turn yourself into a human but you don't know much about how we live, do you," I said, disgusted. "Your failure to erase all traces of your true self is what gave you away."

The lump of flesh that had been Belle, was now nothing more than a shriveled up corpse. Four indistinct limbs jutted from it, but the face of Belle that had melted into Leona's stomach had lost all shape and form. I took a

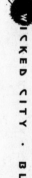

WICKED CITY · BLACK GUARD

shower to clean off all the muck. I glanced back only once as I left the bathroom.

The flesh and bones of Leona's corpse had now transformed into a horrible pool of ugly dark ooze and melted away, all signs of humanity gone.

2

T HE NEXT day, as soon as I arrived at work, I was called into my boss's office. Technically, I had two bosses. One of them paid my salary in the daytime world. An annual 3,700,000 yen including bonuses, made in monthly installments deposited into my bank account. My other boss—whom I referred to only as "Chairman"—was a distinguished, mustached, middle-aged gentleman who assigned me work that paid in amounts ending in six zeros. Usually such work, while profitable, risked not only my life but also my mortal soul. Personally, I had long ago lost track of which man was my real boss, which my real lifestyle.

Both my bosses occupied the same office. My meeting was with Chairman, though. My other boss sat quietly at his desk by the window, absorbed in a thick hardbound book. It was a history of the famous samurai general Tokugawa Ieyasu.

"You've had a little trouble." Chairman's mustached

mouth was smiling, but beyond his stern brow and rigid nose, his eyes were expressionless black holes. *Windows into his soul, perhaps?*

"Just a sucker punch for believing in the Peace Treaty. I almost ended up as another face in her stomach. Was she one of the Militant factions?"

Chairman nodded. "One of the most violent splinter groups. I registered our protest with the Supervisory Section via the Vatican as soon as you contacted me."

"You think a simple complaint will scare them off?"

Chairman shrugged. "The head of the Supervisory Section was very apologetic. They are, after all, a nest of Tranquillities and Peace Front representatives. The problem lies with the Diplomatic Section."

I pressed a finger to my forehead, hard, to try to suppress the headache I'd had since leaving Leona's apartment. Last April had seen some radical personnel changes in the Diplomatic Section. The old, long-standing Head Diplomat retired, and a sharp new youngster had been appointed to his position. Unfortunately, this new head was also highly combative and violent. He was aiming for a reduction in the length of the Peace Treaty, and an increase in length of the Warring Period. The other side had already requested four audiences with our side, and the number of skirmishes was well into three-digit territory.

Chairman leaned back in his seat and glanced at me sideways. I knew something bad was coming. Chairman pursed his lips quickly, perhaps a way to downplay what he was about to say. "They maintain the woman came

WICKED CITY · BLACK GUARD

through mistakenly, was discovered by you and killed without any chance to explain herself. They want us to hand you over. They're also demanding infestation rights around Shinbashi Station."

My face remained impassive. I had almost expected something like this. "And your answer?"

"We're sticking to our guns. You want us to give you up?"

"No."

"However this goes down, you need to be even more careful now. The illegal, uncontrolled crossovers may have been given orders to stir up trouble over here."

"Stuff like this is happening frequently, isn't it? The cases I know of in Tokyo alone run into double digits."

"Today or tomorrow, the worldwide number will hit four digits." Chairman stretched and looked at my other boss. "New York is starting to look like Europe in the Middle Ages. But this is the first time anyone has actually been killed."

"And they claim she didn't intend to kill me? Her attempt to absorb me was just . . . some expression of love?"

"That's exactly what the Diplomatic Section's complaint states." Chairman smoothed his mustache with long, slim fingers. "Remember, we don't have a full understanding of the abilities and emotional expressions of each and every species. That goes double for the dangerous pet troublemakers of the Diplomatic Section."

It was still beyond me to understand why we treated them like humans, assigned them pronouns like *he* and *she*.

In the past, it had been the custom to simply refer to them as *it*. They were not human, after all.

Chairman continued. "There is a reason for this increase in their activity. You must have started to notice it, too."

I nodded. Now we were getting to the real issue. I looked over at my second boss by the window. He was rubbing what little remained of his hair. I always wondered what this man thought of everything that was discussed around him. I have previously spied him pulling his nose hair. Perhaps, with enough observation, I would eventually be able to gauge his level of interest through his mannerisms.

Chairman pulled my attention back to him. "The signing of the next Peace Treaty has been moved up."

My shoulders slumped—so we had come to the real reason for my being here. "A little sudden, isn't it? Wasn't it supposed to be in the fall? They must be going crazy in New York right now."

Sometimes I wondered if Chairman wasn't one of them. In the next instant, I became sure of it. "The location of the signing has been changed, too."

I didn't want to hear what he said next. Really, I didn't, because I knew it would mean nothing but trouble for me. But he kept on speaking anyway, turning my life into a living hell with every syllable.

"For better or worse, the place is Tokyo." He turned his empty eyes toward me, and I wondered if he could read my thoughts, hear the string of epithets I had for him running through my head at that moment.

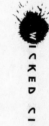

WICKED CITY · BLACK GUARD

"The Megiddo Correctors have confirmed a mistaken reading of the prophecies in the Dead Sea Scrolls. And so the call comes to us . . . to you."

"Our enemies know about the change too, then. And the attack on me makes sense. So who's doing this with me? Did they make it through their attack safely?"

"We believe so . . . or perhaps they just haven't been attacked."

I wasn't expecting to hear that. It was going to be a real big gun, then. "That means it's either 'Great' Ohara from New York or the J. J. brothers from Prague. I've been looking forward to teaming up with both of them."

"I'm sure they'd say the same about you. You'll have to wait to measure cock size, however, because that's not who is coming. This time, you'll be paired with a Guard from their side."

My eyes remained fixed on Chairman's fingers as they stroked his mustache.

"From . . . their side?" I wasn't sure my voice held steady. It was not unknown for us and them to join forces in order to achieve a common goal, but bringing such co-operation about required a substantial amount of power from our side and a fearsome degree of self-control from theirs.

In most cases, even after imposing a huge number of conditions and clauses, the results of such attempts were a complete and bloody failure. Two or three exceptions immediately came to mind.

1966, Pennsylvania: The "spontaneous combustion" of Dr. John Bentley, leaving nothing but his right leg and a slipper. Then there was the monster Rasputin, killed by one of his own kind even as he facilitated the Russian Revolution. . . .

I focused on the task at hand, determined to work with whoever they sent. "Who, then? Do you have his file?"

"Not yet, but it should arrive soon. However, I need you to go to Narita first."

I was a little surprised but didn't show it. "When?"

"Today—right away. Alitalia flight 718 from Rome arrives at four P.M., with Giuseppe Mayart aboard. We need you to keep him safe."

This time I couldn't contain my surprise. Among the Guard, Giuseppe Mayart was a legend, possessed of powerful occult abilities. It was said that Hitler's defeat during the war in Europe was ultimately due to the Führer losing to Mayart in a magical battle. During the planetary alignment of 1982, he was the only thing that prevented the unfolding of terrible things prophesied by mystics across the world.

Having been present at the 1851 Peace Treaty signing, he was said to have then retired to the Apennine Mountains, taking up as quiet a lifestyle as was possible for one of his talents. Or was it Pompeii? For him to be involved now meant this signing was really going to be something. . . .

"As I'm sure you are aware now, the renewal of the Treaty this time is going to mark a new order in relations

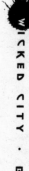

between us and them," Chairman said smoothly. Latent force and expectation rose behind his quiet words. "The period of the new Peace Treaty will be five hundred years."

"Holy shit." The interjection slipped out, but I meant it. The longest Treaty period before this had been from 1851 to 1950, exactly one hundred years. Despite the Treaty, there had been trouble and resistance at every turn, and the First and Second World Wars had occurred, in 1914 and 1939 respectively.

"A long Treaty period is all very well," I commented. "But it means those who oppose it will be all the more focused in their attempts to interfere. The kind of trouble we saw at the last signing could well be about to descend upon Tokyo."

"Which is why we must do all we can to limit the losses. Having discussed it with the top dogs over there, it has been decided that, with the rumors of the signing flying around anyway, the signing should be moved up. It's now slated for tomorrow."

That sealed it for me—Chairman had to be one of them.

"No need to make that face." He showed a rare smile. "Every demon in Tokyo is going to be gunning for you, sure, but we are on even higher alert than normal. You've got one of them on your side, too, don't forget."

I was hardly going to forget that. "I guess he's . . ."

"Oh yes, one of the best they have. *She* is also incredibly beautiful, so I hear."

"She? A woman?" A shiver went up my back that had

nothing to do with the temperature. Partnering up with a woman? I was gonna wind up dead.

"The best way to ensure both the safety and concealment of Giuseppe Mayart is to assign him no more than a pair of highly skilled Guards. You must keep an extremely low profile. I know you can do it." He paused, and I could hear the grin in his voice. "And I have to admit, I'd love to see you two in action out there."

I didn't dignify his obvious teasing with a reply, and he either didn't see or ignored the daggers in my eyes. "The Bureau of Investigations reports quite a number of them have illegally crossed the barrier to our side." The meeting ended with the same words as always. "Best of luck."

My other boss looked up from Tokugawa Ieyasu and waved me over. "Taki, a moment, please. Ohiwa in management had some good things to say about you. The smooth merger with Chuden last month was all thanks to you. I'll be keeping an eye on your progress."

It took me a moment to shift gears and remember what he was talking about. Then I remembered. Oh, yeah—the day job. "Thank you very much." I bowed and left the office, suppressing the urge to take a final glance at my second boss, to see what he was doing.

Soma Chiyako, my bosses' secretary, looked up from behind her steel desk and shot me a smile. But even her beautiful features—she always came out in the top three when the office bachelors took their annual poll of desirable

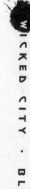

WICKED CITY · BLACK GUARD

women in the office—were not enough to improve my current mood. I thought she might have a thing for me, but just inviting her out for coffee would send unwanted ripples through the office. If word reached the ears of Tachimura in Personnel, my life at work would get a whole lot more complicated. As I headed quietly toward the corridor, her sexy voice followed me.

"Take care out there."

Hardly something you say to the employee of an electronics maker as he ostensibly heads back to his desk. Maybe she had two bosses, too, then?

I wanted to turn back and ask her, but in the end it wasn't worth the trouble, and I left without a word.

3

IT WAS at the fourth Ginza intersection—just in front of the Sanai at the subway exit—that *they* made contact. Their presence was thick and heavy amid the people packed between the concrete buildings. The high walls around us did not help dissipate their force.

A strong tingling ran up the back of my neck, making the hairs stand on end. There were three coming at me from the right—the Mitsukoshi exit. None of them were too powerful, just some green members of a radical faction.

I bought a ticket to Ueno and made my way down to

the Ginza line subway platform. All three followed me. The train drew into the platform, and I thought I was about to be pushed onto the tracks from behind, but the shove didn't come. I got onboard, and even though it was a little past noon, the train was still crowded. They had been using air-conditioners on the platforms for four or five days, but all that did was dry the sweat. At least I wasn't pressed up against other people. The three demons joined me on the train, but I continued to ignore them. At their low level, they wouldn't know I was on to them. All I had to do was lure them somewhere quiet and take them out.

I got off at Ueno, the three pigeons right on my tail. The subway corridors were unexpectedly empty. There was no one up ahead, even though it was the only route to the Tokyo-Narita Skyliner.

I glanced back. Behind me were three youths wearing T-shirts and jeans. I caught some snatches of their conversation, about some girls they had picked up the night before. Following them was a family of three. A forty-something father dragged a massive suitcase along while his wife, dressed in a suit, carried their small baby. That was it. No one else. I looked forward again, noticed a long shadow stretching from the Skyliner entrance on my left. He looked taller than me, and the sleeves of his black jacket reached his knees. Only his T-shirt was white. Everything else, including his bow tie, was black.

A glimpse of handsome, youthful features beneath his wide-brimmed hat stirred my suspicions. It was the kind of beauty few women could profess to.

The youth moved on without looking at me.

I stopped. I had no business with those three. It would be best to let them go by. I faced the wall and retrieved my battered cigarette pack. I took one out and lit it with an old lighter. Cheap cigarettes, cheap lighter. I painted the perfect picture of nothing more than a second-rate salary man.

The voices of the three youths moved past. "I don't think you can turn her down so easily. . . ."

A moment later, the family closed in, and I sensed them moving by, too.

I turned around. The man and the suitcase were already moving on. But the woman had stopped. She stood in front of me, baby to her chest.

Even as I watched, her eyes changed to purple. Before I could do anything, she lifted the baby above her head and smashed it onto the ground. The terrible cracking sound echoed through the corridor, and I wanted to cover my ears. I risked a single glance at the stain spreading across the floor. She seized the moment and attacked.

Her twisted arms spread wide, and something appeared in the vicinity of her chest, ripping through her clothing like it was gossamer silk. White blades like scimitars sliced outward, scattering chunks of red-black flesh onto the floor . . . her ribs. Even though they looked like bones, their tips were honed to fine points, edges as sharp as knives. A terrible weapon that was sure to draw blood no matter where it touched. They stretched out to the left and right, like a mouth ready to stuff me inside.

In the interval between the ribs ripping forth and the woman launching herself at me, I didn't even have time to blink. She looked like some sort of bizarre crustacean or insect, her deadly feelers probing for blood.

With no time to get clear, I felt the rib-fangs close around me like jaws. I raised my arms and blocked them. The woman screamed in surprise. It was the scream of another world, the kind of sound that would drive any normal person insane.

The crushing bear hug of bone teeth squeezed harder. I exhaled and forced my arms apart with all the power I could muster. Like a double door flying open, her upper teeth swung backwards, making a squelching click just before reaching her back. Her jaw slid out of place, the shattered hinges of a door opened too far.

I bent four of my fingers, making them into claws, and thrust them into the exposed windpipe of the womanthing. Then there was the indescribable, terrible feeling of tearing through that flesh.

Guard were trained to attack the head when fighting against demons in hand-to-hand combat because, aside from being the enemy's weakest point, it was the part that felt the most human to the touch. Even the toughest human being who touched a demon's flesh once she had changed would be reduced to a state of dementia for at least three days. Those in a compromised mental state would be plunged into a state of terrifying paranoia, believing all around them were planning their demise, and would use whatever means and weapons they could lay

WICKED CITY · BLACK GUARD

their hands upon to escape. The recent killings perpetrated by street slashers and drug addicts were the result of those people brushing past a demon, touching their arms or skin. It went without saying that the demons caused every one of those incidents on purpose.

Ducking and dodging to avoid the thick, sticky liquid that spewed from the hole torn by my fingers, I slammed the woman's body back toward the Skyliner platform. In their customary fashion, whenever they die, she was already starting to melt. Her body turned into a grayish, sticky mass, which had absorbed even her dress.

Suddenly something punched through the muck. With a fleshy popping, two black spheres burst through the woman's back. For a moment I thought they were eyes, but then they parted down the middle and were drawn back into the remnants of her body via thick sinews attached to them.

Just before they vanished amid the flesh again, I saw tiny rows of what could only be teeth along the edges of the splits. The woman's legs were nothing more than mud on the floor, and I heard the sound of something sucking and slurping the slop.

Those eyeballs were drinking the remains. So they weren't eyes, but mouths.

Beyond the melting woman's corpse stood a teenager in jeans. It was one of the three I had seen earlier. He couldn't have been expecting me to throw the body of his companion in front of his eye-mouths. He'd struck up a conversation with the other two kids from the train, which he must have considered a cunning piece of deception, but it would take more than that to fool me.

The sinews that supported the eye-mouths, perhaps faithful re-creations of the human nervous system, were half white, thicker and darker on the other side. The slow pulsing of these fleshy tubes clearly indicated they were sucking down the womans corpse. They weren't nerves. They were . . . throats, maybe? They extended from the back of the eye-mouths to the kid's eye sockets.

"Wanted a taste of me, did you?" I taunted him, moving into a free stance, preparing for the next attack. The bloody remains of the infant, smashed onto the floor, burned in the corner of my eye, fueling my anger.

He shrugged. "Hey, meat is meat." Even as he spoke, the eyes returned to their home in his eye sockets. The sticky lump, having lost all semblance of humanity, finally crumpled to the floor, its last support removed.

There was less of a splash than I had expected. More than half of her had been eaten, after all. I'd heard the flesh of their own kind was even tastier to them than that of humans.

To humans, of course, it was just disgusting filth, as repellent as feces.

The youth leaped into the air, aiming right for me. He took his head in his hands, and, while still in midair, proceeded to rip it from his neck. Flesh and bone tore, hanging down like tatters of cloth from the shredded stump of his neck, but there was no blood.

There were three ways for demons to disguise themselves

WICKED CITY · BLACK GUARD

as humans. The fastest was to actually alter their skin and bone structure. Demon skeletons differed greatly from human ones, making such transformations extremely difficult and often producing an obvious, mannequin-like result. It also exposed their entire body to attack or damage. Ultimately the tactic was nothing more than a quick fix in emergency situations.

The second method involved bonding a synthetic skin and artificial bones to theirs, and when done well, it could fool even those skilled in clairvoyance. However, creating such a "costume" took a long time.

The third method was the most effective—to simply commandeer and use a human body, as-is. The youth's head retained its shape but instantly took on the pallor of death. The mouth was wide open, its teeth gritted in a single line, when the youth threw it at me.

With a scream like a terrifying bird of prey, the pallid head flew directly at my neck. Another human being killed to serve their sickening ends. I struggled to contain my anger and slammed my right fist into the mouth of the incoming creature. The head's lower jaw opened much farther than was physically possible for a living human, and my entire hand vanished inside it. Teeth dug into my flesh. The lifeless eyes popped out like Ping-Pong balls, and something else—one of the demon's eye-mouths—wound itself around my hand. Pain like burning wire shot up my arm.

Catching me off guard with the head and then deploying his mouth to attack from my blind spot was quite an effective strategy. Anticipating the arrival of the second mouth, I jerked my right arm inward.

The man—or rather, the headless youth—let out a yelp in midair and was dragged off balance. I proceeded to rip out the teeth that were chewing on my arm. Trailing green fluid, the airborne teenager smashed neck-first into the wall behind me. His ankles twisted at an impossible angle, he was reduced to nothing more than a marionette with its strings cut.

Various small mouths still gnashed eagerly, trying to get at my face. I smashed the head into the wall and tore it apart. I closed in on the youth's body. That took care of two of them. Where was the third?

I glanced in the direction of the baby. A white body, almost definitely a demon composite, floated in a sea of blood. The problem was what lurked inside. When the fight began, I'd been pretty sure the baby was the third demon, but something about that didn't quite jibe. The presence that emanated from the remains was off, somehow.

Just as I was trying to figure out what didn't feel right, two sinews, a blue one and a crimson one, slithered across my peripheral vision. Even before I consciously became aware of it, the remains of both the baby and the kid had exploded, and I'd already jumped five meters backwards on pure instinct.

The two sinews melded into one, forming a black sphere the size of a volleyball. Eyes and a mouth appeared, clearly not human, conforming to the physiological laws of the demonic dimension. This was my third attacker.

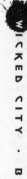

Eldritch and demon blood fused together, the sphere was shaping itself into a body even as I looked on.

Perhaps taking my lack of further movement after leaping away as a sign of fear, a snakelike appendage slithered from the mass and wrapped itself around me, from my ankle to my chest.

The bones in my leg creaked, and I felt such terrible force, enough power to crush the life out of a creature far larger than myself.

The demon smiled. An opening appeared just about where a mouth should be. A single bite was all it would take. There were no teeth inside the mouth—a single suck, then.

It bent its neck backwards, paused, and then shot forward, coming in for the kill. I waited for the strike. And waited.

The demon stopped just centimeters from my face.

I became aware, even during the battle, that a singularly attractive long-coated youth who passed by previously had been calmly closing in on the combat. Now, with expert timing, the youth grabbed the neck of the demon snake, stopping it completely.

"Such a cute little thing, but rather out of place in this world."

Despite being a breath away from death, I was a little taken aback. The voice was a beautiful bell-chime, lingering, haunting. . . . The youth was actually a woman.

With the demon's neck in one hand, she gently stroked the snake's jaw with the other. "Good-bye."

In the same instant that the gentle whisper ended, the snake split like an overripe melon. The beautiful youth . . . beautiful *lady* used her slender white hand to slice the foul mouth cleanly in two.

And I thought my *attacker* had power. The demon's body, seven or eight meters away, was continuing its bloody fusion. It was blown away an instant later. Blood and blue fluid splattered across the floor, the body vanishing from sight amid the gore, dying with a voiceless cry.

"Quite a way to say hello . . . partner." My remark was light as I pulled myself from the split remains of my final assailant, but I knew I was right. There was no way someone with such skills just happened to be passing by. The eldritch snake-human had remained unaware of her presence until it was far too late. I decided to introduce myself and make things official.

"I'm Renzaburo Taki. Just your regular working man."

The woman didn't react. Her thin lips didn't give the slightest indication of even a smile. Her skin, which appeared to shimmer even in this dim light, gave off a sweet, mysterious scent. Combined with the lingering strands of black hair around her neck and cheek, she was replete in her own dimension of ethereal, otherworld beauty.

Even the most beautiful woman in the world would pale in comparison to her, simply because her loveliness was not of this world.

Her first words to me were hardly inspiring. "Not a reassuring performance from my human counterpart. Eldritch snakes are bottom-feeders, nothing more. Those planning the assassination we're supposed to prevent will be far, far stronger than this creature. I fear you will get us both killed."

"I appreciate the honesty," I said wryly. I looked at the eldritch blood covering my clothing. I needed a trip to the little boys' room before buying a Skyliner ticket.

She must have read my mind. "Worried about your clothing?"

"I'd rather you tell me your name."

"My apologies." She sounded sincere about it, too. "Call me Makie. I have no surname. Do you want my vital statistics, too?"

"Maybe later. Glad to see you have a sense of humor, anyway. I bought this suit with my last bonus and wore it for the first time today. I make only 230,000 yen a month, before taxes. You work on this side?"

"As a model."

Should have guessed. She was gorgeous, but I didn't want to weaken my position by acknowledging that to her. "Okay."

"I'm hardly a success. Other models hate me, so I can't get a sponsor."

I could have guessed as much. "We can get to know each other better later. We need to get to Narita. Just give me a moment to wash this gunk off."

Makie nodded. Her manner suited her—professional, elegant.

I took a final look over the scene in the corridor and wondered again why there always seemed to be so few witnesses to my skirmishes with demons. The corridor had been plunged into a demonic vision of hell, but nothing remained except the spreading pools of unpleasantly colored gore. Even they were rapidly fading, leaving no trace that anything out of the ordinary had happened.

PART TWO

1

THE ARRIVAL lobby for international flights, on the first floor of the Narita International Airport's north wing, was still quiet. There was still an hour before the Alitalia flight 718 from Rome was scheduled to arrive. I sat on a sofa near the window, while Makie stood nearby.

"Would you like to sit?" I was being polite, but watching her standing all that time was making *my* feet hurt.

She glanced at the cushioned sofas but didn't move toward them. "No, thank you. I'm unaccustomed to sitting."

I shrugged. It was common among those from the other side not to be able to adapt to our environment, just like some tourists couldn't adjust to exotic cuisine. If I had been invited to sit in one of their chairs, I doubted I could pull it off comfortably the first time. Even for one of their Black Guard, trained in our way of life, the differences between earthly existence and her own constituted a culture shock of epic proportions. Just recently, a veteran Black Guard from their side had managed to blind himself when he mistakenly exposed himself to sunlight. These were minor points, at least when compared with the fact that more than half the humans subjected to the bizarre atmosphere on the demon side were reduced to babbling idiots.

"You see them?" Makie asked quietly.

A group of about thirty tourists passed in front of us. They had arrived half an hour ago on a flight from Greece. It appeared their Japanese contact had yet to greet them, so they were still wandering aimlessly around the lobby.

"Yeah." Of course I could see them. Even if I didn't want to, I could see them. Such skills were what made me so good at my job.

There were two demons hiding among the Greeks. Another sat with those waiting for arrivals, and I spied some among the staff in the wing, too. I could see them all, the otherworldly ones. If anyone else paid enough attention, squinted a bit, they may have seen it, too. The ears of one of the Greeks, a nondescript middle-aged man, were abnormally pointed. On the face of a round tub of a woman in the back in the waiting group, the skin hung oddly. I watched a Japanese couple emerge from one of the shops.

The husband looked okay, perhaps, but the wife's eyes were not large enough given the bone structure of her face. Those two certainly didn't have any children.

These small unsettling *differences* were the kind of thing that would soon be forgotten even if one did take notice of them in the first place. But I could see the truth, their true forms. The alien heart, beating in the crotch of one, and dully glittering eyes inside the mouth cavity of another, his purple blood pumping along narrow veins.

We are not the only ones who walk our streets.

"All these things that we have to see . . . what terrible work we Black Guard do." Makie's comment came out in a tone that suggested she didn't think it was terrible at all.

The first contact between the human and the demon world occurred long ago, understood by the most intelligent representatives of humanity at the time. Having discovered the existence of this *other* place, humanity had made continued contact with the inhabitants of the other side, seeking both exchange and peace between the two worlds. Ultimately, however, they had been forced to accept the fundamental incompatibility of the residents from both worlds. Even if one could become accustomed to their hair-raising appearance—to be fair, each side has the same effect on the other—many demons bore malice, hatred, and an almost overpowering desire to simply wipe us out. That fact of life was pretty impossible to circumvent.

Since the first contact, visitors from the other side had made their way into our world by passageways carved between dimensions, lured by the rich life force and physical phenomena of our world. Tales of the terrible battles between us and them had transformed over the centuries into mere legends and folktales. Tales of man versus demons that all humans knew by name—centaurs, gorgons, the Minotaur, the Kirin . . . All of them faithfully depicted by those who bore witness to the devastation the demons let loose upon our world. The validity of such tales had declined over the years thanks to the Treaty system collaborated on by both sides.

In order to make the system work, humans—through advances in both science and the darker arts—had to develop the ability to cross into the demon world. Just as demons desired human life force and human flesh, so, too, did humans desire the dark magic and supernatural phenomena offered by the demonic realm. Their ability to transmute ordinary matter into gold or jewels was an enviable talent in any century. That was where the rite of exchanging lives for gold stepped onto the stage of history. Humans who made such pacts with demons in order to further their own earthly wealth were known as Demonicas.

As there were humans with bad intentions, there were demons with good ones. Even with the repeated contacts between the two worlds, the main reason our side hadn't been infested immediately was due not only to the instability of the interdimensional passageways, but to the influence of these few well-meaning factions as well. Their fears were ours, and they were well aware of the risk of our side corrupting their world. This was where the idea of the Treaty had come from. It was a noninvasion treaty, covering a number of decades at one time and then renegotiated. Basically, it said both sides would use whatever forces they had at their disposal to prevent anyone from their own world from launching an invasion into the other.

It went without saying that there were those who resisted the enforcement of such a Treaty, demons that sneaked past their overseers to snack upon human flesh, or humans desiring rank, power, and wealth through demonic dealings. On the flip side, there were also a number of voices that called for a peaceful "migration" from their world into ours. Clauses stipulating such things had been added into subsequent contracts, and finally, in 5672 B.C., in the midst of the already legendary Egyptian dynasty, fifty residents from the other side officially migrated to our world after the signing of a new contract in the ruins of Gozo. Since then, the number of immigrants had increased to over five hundred million demons, around a ninth of the total population of the Earth.

Even with such assurances in place, there were still those who sought to take advantage of the situation, along with those who proved unable to resist the temptations of the human realm and who slipped back into their demonic form and ways. There were also many undesirables who forced their way through. Those demons had no desire for a peaceful coexistence, and they dwelled far away

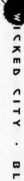

from human cities, deep in dark forests, or in abandoned buildings, attacking humans whenever the chance arose. The key to unlocking the mystery of the annual 700,000 people reported missing in the USA each year lay in the claws of those malevolent demons.

The existence of such creatures, as well as the reality of human beings supporting a series of underworld dealings, could never be revealed to the majority of humanity. It was painfully obvious that if it became general knowledge that anyone—your neighbors, the woman next to you on the train, the man passing you on the street—was potentially a horrifying demon, the revelation would incite panic on a worldwide scale. That was why humans who possessed the talents and skills needed to defeat these inhuman assailants were so vital to keeping the peace. They had the support of demonic agents who could inform them of the actions, abilities, and weak points of those who had crossed over. Of course, this helped immensely. Both demon and human agents learned as much as they could about the two worlds, obtaining the power to deal with demons and the humans corrupted by them. Straddling the human and demonic realms, they were trained and then taught to maintain peaceful coexistence.

Thus the Black Guard was born.

A distant commotion caught my attention.

Seven TVs, mounted at intervals along the wall behind me, each showed a massive crowd of people. It was the news. Though the angle was different on each screen, it was a live or recorded broadcast of the same incident. It looked like Italy, somewhere in the countryside.

I checked the screens out of habit, but professional curiosity made me scan the images of the crowds for anyone—anything—who looked like they might be about to cause trouble of the inhuman kind. All major events on the world stage were assigned skilled units of ten Black Guards. UN representatives, along with the political leaders of each country were, upon appointment, informed of the Black Guard system by my superiors of the highest level.

The camera angle on each TV suddenly matched, perhaps because there was only one camera on the scene. I watched a single black limousine pull into an empty space on the right side of the crowd, and a venerable-looking old man step out. He wore a tall pointed hat and a long white robe.

It was the pope. He had apparently left the Vatican to make a visit to the countryside.

"How majestic," Makie commented. It was impossible to tell exactly how she intended the quiet comment. "I'd much prefer someone like that to protect."

"I don't know much about Mayart either." I thought over the details that I had shared with Makie during the Skyliner ride.

Little was known about Mayart's personality. It wasn't that he was highly secretive, but rather there was just too much conflicting information. He was either a veritable saint, a third-rate Demonica with a big mouth, or the greatest con artist since Cagliostro.

"So long as he isn't some primitive ape."

"Yeah. One thing's for sure—our bosses think he's a big shot."

I turned from the images of the pope kissing a baby and looked toward the arrival gates.

"Shall we go into the waiting room?" Makie was already halfway there as she asked. No one else would have detected the vein of tension in her voice. I followed her. She stopped a step ahead of me down the corridor.

"What is it?" I said.

She went forward again, but more slowly. "I suddenly have a bad feeling about all this."

"An ambush?"

"I don't know. My precognition isn't all that strong. We would need someone who specializes in precognition to know more."

Neither of us actually spoke during this exchange. We used a form of mental communication unique to the Black Guard. The surprise on the faces of those who watched us pass was solely due to Makie's stunning beauty. Her black three-piece suit only served to highlight her sexy figure.

By the time we arrived in the waiting room on the fourth floor, I, too, started to feel something was wrong. A large window overlooked the runway. I sensed the danger was coming from outside. Makie and I stood with our faces practically pressed against the glass, staring out.

A single jumbo jet slowly descended against a fading

blue-pink sky. A Boeing 747. I didn't need to see the letters on the fuselage or the triangle on the tail to know this was the flight we were waiting for. It was just before four.

Mayart was aboard that plane. Two pairs of worried eyes watched as the plane's flaps lowered and the landing gear emerged, preparing the plane to touch down. The plane was only twenty meters above the ground when it happened.

When I recalled the incident afterwards, it seemed that the scream behind me started before anything happened outside. Both wings crumbled—not crumbled, but simply sheared off—as though sliced through by invisible blades, leaving two gaping mouthlike wounds behind them. Even from where I stood, the passengers in their seats became visible.

In the next instant, the nose of the 747 suddenly dipped, smashing into the runway.

At least it was only fifteen meters, which was far better than the ten thousand or more at which the craft normally flew. Sparks and black smoke rose from the place where the nose touched the ground, and a second later, the entire craft was a ball of fire. And then there was a flash that looked like the world had exploded.

Amid the screams, footfalls, and announcements around us, Makie remained composed as she turned toward me. The fireball outside the window looked like a white flower bathed in the evening sun. The sound of the explosion rattled the window glass.

"I hope they don't blame us for this," I commented

wryly. "There was nothing we could have done, anyway. Someone from the Italian side was supposed to accompany him as far as Japan. We don't know for sure he's dead."

Her eyebrows rose slightly. "You think he survived that?"

I shrugged. "I'd best go and make contact. Stay here." I started toward a public phone. An old Slavic man, close to sixty, appeared in front of me, accompanied by a large blond man—his assistant, perhaps?

I made to pass by, but he stepped up in front of me. Some kind of problem? I tried to move around to the left, and he blocked me again.

"What do you want, old man?" I know I sounded aggressive, but I was aggravated at being delayed.

The old man replied in understandable, although thickly accented, Japanese. "Where do you think you're off to? You want to leave the one you're supposed to be protecting alone? You have Carlos here to thank that I'm alive—we took an earlier flight. I do feel sorry for whoever ended up in our canceled seats." He looked me in the eye, smiling at my surprise. "That's right. I'm Giuseppe Mayart. I'm all yours now. Take good care of me!" He gave me a surprisingly white smile.

I looked the old man over. The top of his head reached my neck, around 160 centimeters. His shoulders sloped in an almost feminine way, and he looked remarkably seedy. I didn't much like the look of him. He reminded me of a cunning little rodent, his expression lecherous. His skin had a grayish pallor, his clothing a mess of clashing

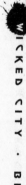

colors—a green jacket and blue slacks. No one else took any notice of him, because of the confusion from the explosion, but by his appearance Makie and I may as well have been protecting a human neon sign.

"I'd heard there was a woman from their side guarding me as well. So?" Mayart asked.

"She's over there. You'll know her as soon as you see her." I pointed toward the window, and those beady rat's eyes of his immediately started to glow.

"I'm going to enjoy this! You, stay here for now." He gave me a final glare and scuttled off in Makie's direction.

I greeted the wryly laughing youth, presumably a Black Guard from Italy, in Italian. "I'm Taki, Tokyo branch." I hitched a thumb toward Mayart. "He's quite the holy man, isn't he? The pride of your country?"

The youth shook his head. "Something like that. I'm Carlos Majarni from the Rome branch. Nice to finally meet you. It's a hell of a long journey, carrying this particular piece of baggage from the Apennines to here. I'm on the next flight back to Rome, but from here on in, the attacks are going to get more violent. There are at least three superpowerful demons among the Militants currently holed up in Japan, and those are only the ones we know about. Watch yourself."

"The old piece of baggage in question . . . he's capable of protecting himself if it comes down to it, is he?" I looked at the small man who capered around Makie. I could hear the disdain in my own voice. My face couldn't have been a pretty picture either.

Majarni seemed hesitant to reply. "I think so. . . ."

"You *think* so?"

"On the way here, we were attacked four times. We killed five of them, lost one on our side, two more injured. At one point, the demons split the road we were driving along in half. Even I thought we were finished, but he didn't show the slightest hint of power. Not once."

"He just left everything to you?"

Carlos nodded. "I don't need to explain. After an hour with him, you'll understand all too well. At least you've got some eye candy along—even if she is one of *them*. Good luck."

We departed with firm handshakes, and I watched his retreating back as he approached the check-in counter. I had a suspicion he would find his fair share of trouble as soon as he got back to Rome. There were just too few Black Guard compared with the number of *them* on the loose.

The sounds of a slap and a yelp turned me around, and I wasn't surprised at what I saw. The scene was like a snapshot out of a farcical comedy—Makie's arm still raised after delivering a cracking slap, the old man ruefully rubbing his stinging cheek. I was the only witness; any other potential audience members were too preoccupied with the tragedy beyond the window to pay any attention.

"What a minx! All I did was say hello!" Mayart jabbed a finger at Makie as I moved closer. His assailant retained her perfect composure.

"What happened?" I asked Makie, though I didn't need to. "His hands get a little too busy for you?"

"Yes."

"What are you talking about? A pinch on the rear is how we say hello in the human world. You there, tell her!"

I gave the yapping old man my best scowl. "I am glad to see that you have so much energy, but please calm down a little. And watch what you say, too. She and I have been dispatched in order to protect your life, even if only for tonight. I have little confidence that I alone can protect you from what is coming. You may do whatever you like tomorrow, but you're stuck with the pair of us for tonight."

"Why you . . . you . . . you little . . . ! Do you know who I am?"

"It doesn't matter who you are," was my crisp reply.

It looked as though Mayart had more to say, but he decided against it and finally clammed up. The eyes he fixed on me were filled with anger, but I paid that no heed.

"Follow us to the Skyliner. Wait, I guess first we should introduce ourselves." I gave him my and Makie's names and, even though it seemed a moot point, welcomed him to Japan. We followed the still bristling Mayart toward the escalators, and Makie said just one thing to me.

"Thank you."

Oh, she's definitely not one of us, I thought again. A young human woman would never say that nowadays.

2

WE LEARNED some of the intricacies of Giuseppe Mayart's overbearing personality on the relatively short ride into Tokyo. It started when a sexy lady, perhaps in her thirties, passed us on the platform.

"A lovely piece of ass," the old goat gloated, taking a swipe at her buttocks as they swayed past.

"I'll feed you to my husband, you little pervert!" was the curt reply.

I crammed Mayart into the Skyliner, already feeling exhausted even though we were only just pulling out of Narita.

"Good work," Makie offered from the seat in front of me. She sat next to Mayart, at the old man's insistence. The slap, the vitriol—nothing seemed to put him off. He was doing pretty well for someone who had to be well over one hundred years old. But her open-palm greeting seemed to be holding him in check, and for now he was behaving himself.

The Skyliner took about an hour to run between Ueno and Narita. It dashed into the deepening dusk, comfortable vibrations running along the carriages. It could lull one into a sense of utter security and peace.

But this was no time to be taking a nap. Makie and I were facing an adversary with the power to take a Boeing

747 clean out of the sky. Confidence was all very well, but underestimating such raw power would be foolish in the extreme. Since we were with Mayart, another such attempt would not succeed. Tragedy on so grand a scale had been possible only because no Black Guard had been on board the plane. If one had been, it would have turned out differently.

The reason we had chosen to use the Skyliner rather than a car for the return trip was because it would prove harder for them to attack with other humans around. It was also easier for them to launch a strike against a car than at a train.

Mayart started his lecherous tirade once more. "I need stimulation at my age. I could drop off the perch at any moment! Can't someone in here strip for me?" He was so loud, that accent or no, the fact he could speak Japanese was going to cause trouble. Nearby passengers had already started to look in our direction. I wondered where he was getting his vocabulary from.

"I could, if you like," Makie said quietly. The fact that it was almost impossible to tell whether she was joking was going to cause trouble, too.

A moment later, the door into the carriage opened, and an attendant came in, pushing a small cart loaded with juice and snacks for sale.

Mayart leaped from his seat. "Whiskey! You got any whiskey on there? I want some Japanese whiskey, largest size you've got. And some squid, too!" He started spouting a list of outdated brands of Japanese whiskeys and telling Makie to buy them.

Makie traded a crisp bill to the girl pushing the cart for some items. Mayart reached up greedily to take them, but I stood and pushed his hands back down.

"What're you playing at now?"

Both Makie and the salesgirl turned their faces toward me in surprise. She really was nothing more than a girl, her face showing traces of acne. I took the whiskey bottle from Makie's hand and thrust it into the salesgirl's face.

"Open this and drink some."

Her mouth fell agape, scandalized. "P-Please, sir, I can't do that."

"Cut that out, you fool! You're embarrassing her!"

I ignored the scattershot Japanese of Mayart's protest and kept my eyes on the girl. I tapped a finger on the cap of the bottle. The girl's face hardened. She knew the game was up.

My impassive expression did not change. "How did you come by that face? Someone make it for you? Or did you just *take* it?" I pressed on the cap, the metal giving a little. "What's behind that face, I wonder? Something not so different from us? Maybe . . . not?"

The girl swept her right hand to the side to fling whatever weapon she had at me. But I was faster, flicking the cap off the bottle. A green line slashed across a bright white flash. Before I could react, something ripped through the salesgirl's chest. A hand, far larger than my own and

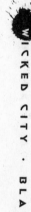

with copper-colored nails, erupted from the shredded flesh and grabbed the salesgirl's neck. With a meaty squelch, the flesh of her throat was squeezed together. The blood that fountained out was green-blue in color.

The demon salesgirl's body slumped against me. The hand, however, hadn't died with the rest. It reached desperately for Makie's throat, revealing an attached arm as it did so. Makie's face hardened slightly, and her white hand closed around the attacking arm.

There was no need to cast so far as the fanciful tales of the genie in Aladdin's lamp to find examples of matter being stored in a space where it was physically impossible for it to fit. However, such a process required the supernatural ability to alter the physical properties of the item in question and then maintain its basic essence while adjusting its shape in order to succeed. If said item happened to be a living creature, the pain that accompanied this process was beyond imagination. A living creature sealed up in this way would eventually be consumed with hatred and suffering, fed only by the bile of its degenerating mind, waiting for hundreds, even thousands of years. That long-fermented hatred would direct itself at all living things on the outside, and in many cases the one who finally freed them—be it intentionally or not—was often the first to die.

This hand, with its nails the color of new coins, must have suffered the same pain, the same suffering. The first things it had come across in its freedom were the salesgirl . . . and Makie. The flesh on Makie's neck did not tear so easily. Her white fingers gripped the hand and then bent one of those ugly fingers backwards. She held her attacker back with her left hand and snapped a finger with her right. She took the thumb and bent it back so that it was level with the back of the hand.

The hand trembled. The blood vessels beneath the skin swelled, the remaining fingers clawing at the flesh of Makie's throat. It looked like Makie was almost enjoying herself.

Her elegant hand now held the index finger and bent it backwards, too. It didn't look as though she was straining very hard, but the thick, ugly finger easily bent all the way back.

A slight smile curved Makie's lips. She was enjoying it. She was a demon, all right.

The hand now tried to go back into its bottle—the salesgirl's ruined body. Makie took the middle finger. *Crack.* The ring finger made the same dull crack. Once she snapped the pinkie, all power faded from the hand, and it flopped over, lifeless as wax.

"You poor thing," Makie whispered as she tossed the hand onto the already melting body of the girl. Blue-green fluid splashed with a thick, sickening squelch, and the hand sank sullenly into the girl's chest like a dog in a quagmire.

All eldritch and demonic beings that died on our side were reduced to this sticky mess in an average of three

seconds. Because of this rapid disintegration, there was no definitive answer to the question of what made them so impervious to almost all of our weapons. Maybe it was their tough hides, or their powerful life force. Whatever it was, I wasn't going to find the answer in the gooey mess on the floor of the Skyliner.

Makie turned to Mayart. "Everything is okay," she said quietly. Mayart hung on the edge of his seat, his face the color of old porridge.

"What . . . what are they thinking? . . . I'm just here to sign the Treaty!"

"Sorry for the mess." I took a small cologne bottle filled with odor-neutralizing spray from the pocket of my suit and sprayed a little around. The terrible stench of a demon's melting body was enough to send regular humans into mental chaos. The smell lasted only about thirty seconds, though, and if the melted remains were collected and preserved in a certain manner, they could be used to create a powerful medication for schizophrenia.

Black Guard regulations stipulated that as much of the substance as possible should be gathered at every available opportunity, but now was not the time. The terrible stench hung in the air, melted flesh bubbling. It rapidly disappeared, leaving no sign of the struggle between us.

Mayart was still ranting. I placed a finger against the old man's lips. "Please, keep quiet. Our enemies may still be among the passengers. We cannot let our guard down."

He calmed down, but there was still panic in his eyes. "I'm getting off. Stop the train."

"This is nonstop."

Mayart slumped dejectedly in his chair. I watched him from the corner of my eye and turned toward Makie.

She shook her head slowly. "Troublesome old man."

"Yeah, but his lewd behavior doesn't match his status, if you know what I mean." I shrugged. It was pointless to try to figure him out. "Anyway, I managed to catch the salesgirl's presence before she could do any damage, but can you sense anyone else?"

"I don't think so."

"We will once we arrive in Ueno, I'm sure."

Makie nodded. "The Militants are really pushing hard." A shadow lurked behind her light tone, like there was something terrible she didn't want to mention.

I leaned against the seats. "How can you tell?"

"We know there are at least three super-class demons on our trail. Their modus operandi is pretty much to smash whatever is in their way with all the power they have. Whether one at a time or all three, once they realize we're putting up a fight, they'll send in the best they have. The salesgirl was tougher than those three you and I ran into before, but she is still nothing compared to those we must face in the hours ahead. The gradual escalation in the power of the demons they're sending is to test how strong we are."

"Hmmmm." I tapped my forehead lightly. The demons we had fought so far were strictly small-fry. They had

WICKED CITY · BLACK GUARD

fangs and claws enough to prevent any fisherman from mistaking them for bait. "What can you tell me about the powers the three Supers have?"

"Nothing." Makie slowly shook her pretty head, and an impossible fragrance wafted from her hair and filled my nostrils. Perfume from our world rarely suited those of the demonic persuasion, but when it did, it blended with their natural scent to make an ethereal aroma.

She obviously didn't notice the effect it had on me, because she continued without missing a beat. "The abilities of each of them are top secret. Internal fighting is still rife among the Militants. However . . ."

"However?"

"Let me put it to you this way—one of them could easily wipe out the entirety of Tokyo all by himself."

I got it, even though I didn't want to. "Like a tactical nuke . . . equal to a three-megaton blast."

"I said it would be easy for them."

"Whatever. They're still too much for me." My shoulders slumped as I draped myself over the back of the chair.

We were somewhere around Funabashi. The lights of the peaceful city flowed past the window, distant and untouchable as stars.

Regardless of how our enemies had evaluated our abilities, the Skyliner made it into Ueno without any further trouble. We exited, Mayart following us with a stiff, set face. It was a fine change from his endless complaining.

We transferred to the subway as carefully as possible, watching for attacks from all sides. It was easier for demons to take possession of others in subway passageways, small alleys, or other dark enclosed places. They preferred it because they could gradually change their surroundings so to mimic their natural environment. That was why many people experienced a shudder or chill when entering an underground parking lot or seemingly empty corridor. The spate of abhorrent incidents involving children being abandoned in coin lockers were actually demands being made by their side. A bomb unit would be deployed to sweep the lockers, and a terrible smell would fill the locker and subway, driving everyone out while the demons picked off their prey.

While it was easier for them to take possession in such places, it was also easier to sense them there, because their presence became more concentrated. Even for a demon who could elude a skilled Black Guard out in the open, once they entered an enclosed space, it was like they were playing rock music at full blast. Any kind of surprise attack became impossible. Which made it easier to handle them, at least from our point of view, and it generally avoided the trouble of having to deal with large numbers of witnesses. Taking the subway was less risky than driving in a car on the open streets. The three who attacked me at the start of my trip were too weak and inexperienced to understand these subtle maneuvers.

We boarded the subway at Ueno. The trip to Ginza went peacefully. There were demons among those in the train with us, but only a few, and they didn't seem to pay us any heed. Most demons, Militants or not, would be staying in their holes until the signing was over. They didn't want to get caught up in any trouble. Those we sensed on the train had probably been exposed to the atmosphere on this side for too long. When that happened, they lost sight of what they truly were, thought of themselves as humans. This happened often to those demons with a low demonic disposition.

We left the subway, and Mayart, without a care to our need for traveling incognito, piped up loudly, "So this is the world-famous Ginza! Never thought I'd ever see it outside of photographs."

"You have impressive knowledge of Japan," I said with a sardonic look.

"Don't mock me!" Mayart warned. He gnashed his pointed little teeth. "My hideaway in the mountains has a fully stocked library. Now, since we're here, I'd like to take a stroll around Ginza!"

I scratched my ear. "Yeah, I guess we can do that. But we don't have much time."

"Hah! It isn't even six thirty yet. Don't tell me you planned on going straight to the hotel and locking me away for the night? Unacceptable! I'd be out the window and in the next titty bar before you could blink!"

I gave Makie an exasperated look, which she returned with a calm, reassuring one. "It should be okay. I doubt they'll attack us in the middle of Ginza."

I curled my lips in exasperation. "What a tough old bastard."

"Have you two got something to say?" Mayart chided. "If not, then let's go. I'm eager to see everything."

We soothed the old man's complaints and started out along Ome Street, heading toward Hibiya. The activity in Ginza was no different midweek than it was on a Saturday, especially around the fourth intersection, Hibiya Park and Ome Street, which led to the outer gardens of the Emperor's palace. Our lodgings were close to the Imperial Hotel, so we were taking the long way around to get there.

Although Makie and I wore practiced neutral expressions, every nerve in our bodies was taut, on edge. The same could not be said for Mayart. He was delighted by everything he saw. He expressed his awe at every opportunity—in English, surprisingly.

"How beautiful. How amazing!" His cries drew laughter from passersby.

We had just passed Akebono and Kondo Books when a pair of glamorous Latinas appeared in front of us. I looked them over—nothing. They were human.

Mayart walked right up to them. "Grazie, grazie." The girls looked as confused as I was. None of us had any idea what he was thanking them for, and I wondered if he was even really Italian. Regardless, his impudence was matched only by his skill with the ladies. The more attractive of the two women gave the old man a saucy smile, and my instincts flew into overdrive.

A demon? No. Human? Yes. Weapons? None. Dangerous? Oh yeah, without a doubt.

I was moving almost before I reached the end of my train of thought. The girl was about to place her arms around Mayart. I grabbed the old man's collar and dragged him away. The glamour girl's hand snapped shut, like the mandibles of an insect, but Mayart was already out of danger.

Mayart wasn't amused. "What are you playing at?" Obviously he hadn't realized what was happening or that I had just saved him. Before he had even finished his angry shout, the street in front of us started to glow. The girl suddenly spewed fire. More than fire; it was like a miniature nuclear explosion. The flames did not expand outward, though, and there was no smell of burning flesh. Even so, waves of heat rippled away from her body and set the second girl aflame. Sparks showered onto the clothing of passersby, and the blast's shock wave brought a billboard crashing down across the street. The silhouettes of fleeing people were burnt onto the walls and street, as if they had been painted.

Amid the pandemonium, the screams, and fear of the people trying to escape, the shining mass suddenly blinked out. She wasn't just burnt to the bones, there was absolutely nothing left of the pretty girl.

I had to get Mayart out of here before law enforcement arrived. "This way, quickly!" I pushed Mayart into action, Makie following behind.

"Body-burning. That's extreme," Makie whispered. "That poor girl must have drunk something combustible without even knowing it."

I tossed an incredulous look over my shoulder as we fled the scene. "That was a nuclear explosion."

Makie gave a short nod. "Biologically speaking, the human body is nothing more than an energy-burning engine. If you induce excitation of nuclear division or super-accelerate the reaction when oxygen and hydrogen combine to form water inside the human body, it's not impossible to cause such a reaction. The human body has been a field of research on our side for a long time now."

"Like Mary Reeser . . ." I whispered the name of the most famous victim of spontaneous human combustion. A seventy-seven-kilo, sixty-seven-year-old woman from Florida, Mary H. Reeser departed this mortal coil in a mysterious localized conflagration on the morning of July 2, 1951. Mr. P. M. Carpenter, resident of 1200 NW Chili Street, Petersburg, in the same state, arrived at Mrs. Reeser's room that morning to share a cup of coffee and, when he reached for the brass doorknob, burnt his hand. The metal was hot.

Mr. Carpenter found help in the form of a painter working nearby. Together they entered the building and found Mrs. Reeser sitting in the midst of an eddy of swirling, hot, fetid air. Or rather, they found the remains of Mrs. Reeser. The only thing that indicated she had once been human was one of her feet, still in its slipper,

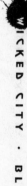

found after they had dug through the remains. The rest of her ample form had been reduced to charcoal and ashes.

The coroner's examination revealed that, aside from the foot, the only other parts of the departed lady to keep their shape were her skull, which had shrunken to the size of a baseball, her burnt liver, and part of her spine. Mrs. Reeser's seventy-seven-kilo body had been reduced to a pile that weighed less than four kilos.

It takes heat between 3,000 and 3,500 degrees to burn bones. In the case of Mrs. Reeser, everything within a fifty-centimeter diameter, including the carpet, had melted. But a pile of old newspapers just outside the burn radius remained totally untouched.

Edward Silk, the coroner, eventually ruled it an accidental death, cause unknown. Dr. Wilson Copeman of Pennsylvania University also took a look at the case, but eventually threw in the towel, unable to explain how a fire capable of shrinking Reeser's skull and consuming her body had initially ignited.

The FBI released a report, stating that Mrs. Reeser, a habitual user of pills to help her sleep, had drifted off while smoking and her gown had then caught fire. No one believed it—there was no way that a conflagration started by a cigarette could reach 3,000 degrees. The truth of the incident remained shrouded in mystery.

Mrs. Reeser's certainly wasn't the first case of its kind. The phenomenon began to garner attention somewhere around the mid-eighteenth century, with numerous detailed examples printed in Charles Dickens's novel *Bleak House*. Most of the victims were elderly, infirm, or widowed, which led a number of police departments to initially suspect suicide, but that didn't offer an explanation as to how the fire started. Other theories had been floated over the years, from alcohol as a catalyst, psychic murder, and a static electric spark, all of them potentially reasonable explanations. In reality, however, the most insane explanation was actually closest to the truth.

It was the demons.

According to investigations, the mid-eighteenth century was also when research of the human body by the other side was at its most prolific. Strange though it may sound, there was a fierce debate among demons concerning the cruelty with which humans were killed. After evaluating the tried and tested methods of tearing them apart or eating them alive, more "humane" methods were proposed. Like spontaneous human combustion. Nice, huh? Glad they were thinking of our feelings when they came up with that one.

Anyway, here we were, walking away from a human nuclear bomb. Mayart was too shaken to walk, so Makie and I held him under each arm and finally made it out of the blast zone. We headed toward Hibiya and turned toward the film district. We had passed a large theater, and the sign for our hotel came into view. Even residents of Hibiya did not know about the small two-story brick building tucked away behind the old wing of the famous

WICKED CITY · BLACK GUARD

Imperial Hotel. The odd drunk might stumble into the place every now and then, but the stern-looking man who worked the front desk would deter them from staying.

I pushed through the revolving door and was immediately confronted by said cast-iron gentlemen, his round glasses glinting in the lights of the lobby.

I preempted his attack. "No need to put the scare on me. We've got a reservation."

He hadn't even moved from his place behind the desk. "I know. Second floor, room thirteen."

I sent Makie and Mayart further into the lobby. "Any other guests?"

"No need to worry. Just you three."

"What about guards?"

He blinked behind his glasses, looking like an overgrown insect. "You two and me aren't enough?"

"You would think so, but some pretty big players are making moves on the other side. Even if this is an Impenetrable Designation, I can't guarantee we'll be totally safe."

The hotel owner breezed through the door behind the desk. "The barriers are at triple strength." He brought the leather-bound guestbook and a quill pen over to me. "And we are not without armaments here. Take your pick. I've got some real historical pieces stashed here."

"Just a revolver will do. Something powerful, even if it's a little large. Some ammo, too. You got *treated* bullets?"

"What do you think?"

I nodded. "Good." As I filled out the guest register, I was struck by an urge to check the names written on the first page of the guestbook. Everyone who stayed here experienced the same feeling, an itch that could easily be scratched by simply flipping back through the pages. As of yet no one had dared to try it. Rumor was that the name Jesus was inscribed on a square of papyrus. The truth of this remained unclear, but the names of noted personages like Deguchi Onisaburo and Edgar Cayce had been confirmed among those on the later pages.

I took the brass key and headed up the elegant spiral staircase to our suite on the second floor. Mayart was already well into his temper tantrum by the time I arrived.

"Look at this place! Tiny!"

Makie gave him a patient sigh. "We will be staying with you all night. It's the best we can do."

"Hah!" Mayart tilted his head to the side. "I veto that little decision. I don't mind the lady, but I'm not spending the night with you." He pointed a long fingernail at me. "I can't sleep with a man in the same room!"

I remained cool. "Then you will have to stay awake."

"What!" Mayart's face filled with rage.

The signing was scheduled for 5 A.M. the following morning. It was seven o'clock now, meaning we had ten hours to kill, probably literally. Ten hours of concentrated enemy attack. As long as we were inside the hotel, everything should be all right.

Mayart's tirade continued. "I'm a VIP. Without me, there is no Treaty. You're forcing me to stay in this cheap

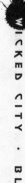

dive. This is abuse. How dare you! I'm going to complain to the head of the Tokyo branch!"

"The very purpose of this hotel is to protect VIPs like yourself," I said through gritted teeth. "Powerful spirit walls surround us. There is a strong center of spiritual power located directly beneath us. Lower-level demons won't even be able to come close to this place, let alone get inside."

"If that's so, how come she was able to waltz right in?" Mayart jabbed a disgruntled finger at Makie.

"She is one of the Black Guard. She has received extensive training, and has permission to enter."

"Huh. Very well, I'll stay with her. But first you are going to take me to Roppongi, then to a club."

"You will refrain from leaving this room, for tonight."

His ashen face turned purple with anger. "You little runt . . . ! Who the hell do you think I am?"

His fixed me with blazing eyes. I stared back with a blank expression, and he quickly backed down. He had sensed the difference between an old man who lived in seclusion in the mountains and someone who faced demonic combat on a daily basis—a gaping chasm of difference.

Mayart turned and sat quietly in a chair. So childlike, for all his advanced years. "Very well. I will stay with you."

I was about to cut in again, but Makie shut me down. "Very good, thank you. So long as you understand."

Mayart's face immediately broke into a huge grin, his greedy eyes roving freely over Makie's body. "So, get out." He meant me. "You can't stay here. Go find a sofa to sleep on." He suddenly seemed to change his mind. "Or, you could stay. Having someone watch turns me on even more. We could even enjoy a little threesome?"

I looked to Makie for a decision.

She waved me out the door. "I'll be fine. I'll let you know if he tries anything. I wouldn't want it getting back to my bosses, either."

Mayart cackled. "She knows the way of things, doesn't she. I have to admit, I love to kiss and tell."

I sighed, but then gave a nod. "As you wish. But keep an eye on him."

"Understood." I trusted Makie's quiet confidence. Having been dismissed, I returned to the lobby. I asked the hotelier to set me up with another room and sat in a high-backed chair, glancing around the room, which was hardly large enough to warrant the moniker *lobby*.

I retrieved a cigarette from my pocket and lit up. Smoke flowed into my lungs, and within a few seconds, my entire body relaxed, the tension in my nerves eased so long as I held in the smoke. Everything returned to normal as soon as I exhaled.

The owner returned, adjusting his tie. I didn't know anyone whom a black suit and bow tie suited as well as this man. He carried a paper bag, and the sound of metal objects clicking together came from inside it. He placed the bag on the scratched ebony table.

After a quick check of the curtains to make sure they

were all drawn closed, I took a look inside the bag. The proprietor sat in the chair opposite me, watching intently. I pulled out a dully glinting weapon that certainly didn't look like something a human could use. But the six-shot, high-caliber revolver, with an elegant barrel that totally ignored even the vaguest idea of portability, and sturdy walnut grip, almost felt as if it had been made for my hands.

A Smith & Wesson M29 .44 Magnum. It was the most powerful handgun on Earth, and the height of human innovation in weaponry. I pressed the cylinder latch and swung it open. Six black holes stared back. I returned the cylinder, pointed the gun at the ground, and pulled the trigger. The trigger was double action, three kilos. I didn't know who had made the alterations, but I liked their style. I squeezed until the instant the striking hammer was about to fall and then released. I practiced this ten or so times, getting a feel for the gun.

I took a box of fifty Winchester hollowpoints from the bag, opened it, and plucked out six to load into the cylinder. The bullets were tipped with silver. Vicious little bastards, the impact would compress them to almost three times their initial diameter within the body of the target for massive damage.

I closed the cylinder and checked the overall gun balance, making sure the striking pin wasn't crooked before sliding it into my shoulder holster. I had no love for the fashionable nylon holsters, so mine was worn, used leather, and it gently received the weapon as a mother might take her child.

"Anything for the lady of the house?" I asked.

"Keep looking."

In the bottom of the bag was a Beretta M84 automatic, sporting a fifteen-round clip. Its grip was a little fat; it was only a midsized automatic, a little small to feature double-action, but nothing that Makie's fingers couldn't handle. The magazine was empty, but the two clips in the bag were already loaded with .9 silver points. There was a black leather shoulder holster, too. The thought of this weapon beneath Makie's clothing was oddly stimulating.

There were another two boxes, fifty rounds each, and a cleaning kit and some gun oil.

"Thanks for all this."

The owner nodded in response. "Nothing more than toys given what you are up against. But you need whatever advantage you can gather, eh? There's no guarantee you won't face human thugs, either. Try not to kill too many poor punks. Dying is for demons."

I removed my jacket and hung the M29 from my shoulder. A chill crept through the leather and then my shirt, sinking deep into my skin. That sensation was proof the gun had been "treated" to handle demonic encounters.

"How is your wife?" I asked suddenly. This was the only way I knew to crack the hotel owner's stony visage, the perfect question to ask a henpecked husband.

It worked liked a charm. "She . . . she's in the back, exercising or something. Let's not talk about her, shall we?"

"A little aerobics, huh?" I smiled slyly, pressing the remaining stub of cigarette down into the ashtray. Budget smokes were a lifeline to someone on such a cheap salary as mine.

"Our VIP is Giuseppe Mayart, correct?" The owner's face turned stony once more.

"Yep. In the flesh. You ever met him before?"

"Just once. About twenty years back, he sneaked into Japan for a little business, a little pleasure. He hasn't changed much."

So it really was him. The owner's next comment shredded my previous thought into confetti. He looked at the ceiling, pensive. "Although, I can't be sure you're escorting the real deal."

The flame on my cheap lighter wavered as I attempted to light another cigarette. I replied from the unoccupied side of my mouth. "What do you mean?"

The hotelier shrugged. "Just a hunch. It's the hunch of a man who has been dealing with guests here since you were knee-high." He smiled and waved his hand, brushing away the thought. "I've nothing to prove he's definitely someone else, either. Pay me no mind."

I sucked down a lungful of smoke.

So our Mayart was a decoy? Such a diversion made sense—the real Mayart would show up for the signing in a different place, at a different time . . . meanwhile, all the demons who wanted Mayart dead would be focused on us.

It was just like Chairman to pull something like this. Sleight of hand backed by a performance that could bring down the house.

The question was, how did this new information change things for us? I thought for a moment and looked at the owner. "Don't tell anyone else about any of this."

The owner nodded. "I take it the demons will be paying us at least one visit tonight anyway?"

"I presume so. They know we came in here. They can't just walk in themselves, however. So they'll try to break through. You'd do well to boost the barriers."

"I think I'll enjoy a break in the monotony." The owner's narrow eyes glittered behind milk-bottle lenses. "They tried to break through before. Just once, must be almost thirty years ago now, back when my father was still around. Gurdjieff was staying here. I still remember what it felt to snap one of their necks with my bare hands. Bring it on."

"I'll be counting on you." I made to stand.

"Still not married, eh?"

The question shook me a little. "That easy to tell?"

The owner studied me with a penetrating gaze. "What about her upstairs?"

"She's from the other side. One of them."

"Hey, you don't need to tell me. I knew as soon as she walked in here. So what's wrong with that? Even if you can't have kids, I hear the sex with them is fantastic."

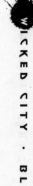

"Don't get excited, it's not happening." I stood abruptly and left. I arrived back at Mayart's room and knocked loudly on the door.

Makie appeared almost immediately. She looked exactly as I had left her.

"A little something." I passed her the bag with the gun and bullets.

She peered inside. "So thoughtful. Thanks."

I lifted my chin toward the back room. "What's our old friend doing?"

"I won't play along, so he's reading a magazine. They have a feature on hot spots in Tokyo."

I smiled. "Just keep an eye on him."

"I will. One night shouldn't be too tough." There was a strange sparkle in her eyes I didn't understand.

"Something up?"

"No, it's nothing. Good night."

The door closed before I could reply.

That quiet click was accompanied by gunshots downstairs. With a shout to Makie to stay in the room, I rushed back down.

The demon presence hit me the second I reached the first floor. It didn't take long to figure out where it was coming from, either. A middle-aged man in a medium-quality suit ran toward me, the smoke boiling from his neck and throat indicating the price he was paying for being inside the spirit walls.

The man saw me and swung with a right hook. I blocked the attack. As soon as the limb touched me, it turned into a deadly claw. I slammed my fingers into the assailant's throat, killing him instantly. I kept my body low to the floor and made a dash for the lobby. Four more bodies lay on the floor, three of them liquefied. Three more shadows lurked in the open doorway. I spied the shadows of the owner and his wife behind the counter, their figures outlined by the blazing flame of gunfire they aimed at the remaining threat.

Two of the three demons were downed instantly, but the third leaped easily and impossibly high into the air. He landed smoothly in front of me. He looked like another average man, but the arms that grabbed my shoulders had the power to shatter my bones. I slammed my head forward into his, and he jumped back. His head—which was apparently just for show—ripped from his shoulders and soared into the air. Something decidedly inhuman pushed through the torn-off hole.

It looked something like a centipede—except that the eyes on the end of its head were full of obvious intelligence . . . and hatred. It used the limbs that jutted from the sides of its body to slide partially out of the headless torso before attaching itself to my leg like a leech. There was the distinct feeling of something flowing into my body—the bug was injecting me with God only knew what. My body reacted before I could even think, and I jerked my knee. As it pulled away, I felt the demon's flesh tear open. But the demon who controlled it would feel every bit of the pain.

The master emerged completely from the man's body.

Without its master inside, the body lost its power. I ripped its arms free from my shoulders. The suit tore open with a horrible splitting sound, and the man dropped to the floor, shreds of skin flapping.

The weakened centipede demon attempted to crawl away across the floor. I stamped on it as hard as I could. As it died, the creature spewed a string of what I figured were words.

"Are you okay? All in one piece?" The hotelier dashed to my side, his Browning HP dangling from his right hand.

"I'm fine. . . ." I managed to mutter through the pain. My internal Psy Power was currently running detox on the eldritch fluid the demon had injected me with. Two seconds later, I was fine again. I sensed a familiar presence and looked toward the stairs. Makie stood there.

"I told you to stay in the room. . . ." Something wasn't right. "What happened?"

Makie looked abashed. "Mayart got away."

I dashed up the stairs, pushing past Makie. I burst into the room. Although the hotel showed many signs of its age, the bathroom and toilet were exceptions to the rule— they looked brand new. The bathroom door was open. So was the small window inside.

Makie came up behind me. "As soon as the shooting started, he shouted something about hiding and ducked in there. I didn't know there was a window. It's my fault."

"You think?" I crossed the bathroom and looked out

the window. It was about two meters square, a rectangle that would have been tough for most grown men to squeeze through. I looked up and saw the stars. The road, ten meters below, marked the perimeter of the Imperial Hotel.

"He jumped from here? Crazy old guy. He must really want to get his rocks off. Roppongi, was it?"

"He'd marked a red circle in the magazine he was reading," Makie said. "Well, I presume he can read Japanese."

"As well as thirty or more other languages, supposedly. You remember the name of the magazine?"

Makie replied with the name of some small-time men's weekly that I was only vaguely familiar with. "Getting the inside scoop, huh. What about the name of the place he marked?"

"I didn't pay careful attention. But I remember the general area on the map."

"We need a copy of the magazine."

"What should we do?"

I snorted impatiently. "We'll have to start by finding somewhere that sells it."

"I doubt a normal bookstore carries that title."

She wasn't being helpful. "Maybe a vending machine, then. Stupid old man!"

We headed into the corridor. The hotel owner, now wearing a rubber apron and long boots, was mopping up the slime from the battle in the lobby. The grip of his

Browning HP jutted from the apron pocket. A large plastic bucket stood next to him, full of clothing covered in red-black globs.

"What're you going to do with their clothes? Burn them?"

"Hey, they're my size," the owner replied. He was apparently going to wash and then wear them.

I shook my head in amusement and dropped the subject. "Is there a magazine vending machine around here?"

The owner stopped his cleaning and leaned on his mop. "A few, next to the old Hibiya Theater. Hey, you want a beer?"

"No. I need something a little more adult."

He looked at me carefully for a moment and then said, "You can get that there, too."

I asked him to find me a change of clothes and headed outside. Makie followed.

The streets were still busy with pedestrians. I watched them cautiously and lit another cigarette. "He's got some balls, that old guy. No matter how much he likes women, I'd thought he'd be cowering under a blanket once the fighting started."

Makie looked both ways as we crossed the street. "He's certainly got confidence in something, hasn't he?"

That was for sure. So was ours the real Giuseppe May-art? Or just some sex-crazed old man?

We found the vending machine exactly where the owner had said we would. "None left." Makie finished looking over the rows of vibrant magazine covers. Her mechanical and yet somehow alluring sexy words struck a most out-of-place chord within me.

I missed what she had said, drawn away by my own thoughts. "What?"

"The magazine, of course."

The cover of the magazine was there, amid the assorted erotica, but there was a red lamp next to the price. Sold out.

"We'll have to try something else." Makie turned away.

"Hold on, wait a second."

"There's no point, Taki."

"There's still one here. I'm going to get it." I told Makie to step back and placed the palm of my hand against the glass of the vending machine. It took only a moment to measure the thickness—about two millimeters. I put every ounce of force in my body into the palm of my hand, disturbing the surface tension of the glass.

My personal power was like a negative magnetic field, able to influence the bonding of molecules. It was fairly easily to accomplish this phenomenon through modern scientific means, but in my case, I could also influence the composition of those molecules from the other side, too.

In layman's terms, I had a type of Psychic Power. Just as I could slice through five reinforced, fire-resistant bricks with a single chop, I could also shatter demonic bones, which were said to be able to resist high-caliber cannon fire. My fingers could jab into their throats, and I could destroy them with a power beyond even the laws of

WICKED CITY · BLACK GUARD

their bizarre realm. All usual forms of force could not bring death to a demon, which was the reason for the formation of the Black Guard.

Once I used my Psy Power, it took less than a second for the glass to turn into fine powder, glittering in the lights of the vending machine. I had just grabbed the dirty magazine from inside when footsteps approached from behind.

"Hey, what're you doing there?" The overbearing tone identified the speaker before I even turned around. Not a demon, but two policemen making the rounds.

"I asked, just what are you doing?" the older of the two men repeated angrily. The younger one noticed the hole in the vending machine.

"Look at this hole. . . ." He glanced at the magazine in my hand. "That's quite a thing to steal."

The older officer extended his hand toward my wrist. "Come with us." Before he could touch me, there was a light *thwap,* and the man collapsed to the ground as though his bones had been turned to mush.

I had done nothing but rap him lightly with the quickly rolled up magazine.

"What the hell . . . ," the second man started, dashing in, but I easily dodged him and then smacked his exposed back with the magazine. I guess being called a thief bothered me more than I thought, because the blow was stronger than I intended. The unfortunate policeman flew almost three meters and crumpled to the ground.

Having authority tended to make human beings feel

full of themselves; hopefully this encounter would bring these two victims of such aggrandizement down a notch or two.

We hurried back toward the hotel, flicking through the magazine as we went. "This page . . . here." Makie's long, elegant white finger pointed to our next destination.

PART THREE

1

THE TAXI stopped in front of a cavalcade of glaring neon signs blazing in primary colors. Next to a jacketed pamphleteer hawking fleshy wares, placards proclaimed ALL THE TOUCHING YOU LIKE and ECSTASY GUARANTEED. The place looked pretty popular—two businessman types disappeared inside as we watched.

"A strange place to pick . . . all the way out in Kamata." Makie's mouth formed a light smile. I couldn't help but chuckle, too.

"Quite a fall from the heights of Ginza."

"Do you think they'll let me in?"

"We can say you are an overly beautiful drag queen."

"I hope they don't demand proof. Let's go."

We left the cab and walked through the door, calls of "Come in, come in!" drawing us toward the entrance. Even the loudmouthed hawker, getting on in years, considering his profession, was briefly at a loss for words when he caught a glimpse of Makie. His jaw hung open, slack flesh wobbling. That was the sheer power of Makie's beauty.

As soon as we entered the place, the smell of smoke and cheap liquor hit us. The air was colored with it. The wide floor was jammed with sofas and tables, the heads—and other parts—of men and women poked from the sofas at various angles. The whole scene was backed by heavy rock music and the calls of men and women. I looked around the bar but didn't see our pigeon.

Makie's eyes were sharper than mine. She tapped my shoulder and then pointed into the thin darkness, and I saw the ratty, laughing face we were looking for. Even though it was dark, I could see as clearly as if it were daylight.

Mayart's face froze when he saw us standing at his table. His expression was almost one of hatred, as though Makie and I were his worst enemies. One girl sat at his side, and two more sat opposite. All three looked at me suspiciously. As soon as their gaze moved to Makie, their suspicion turned into jealousy. Makie did not even acknowledge the three girls, which probably made them mad as well as jealous.

"How the hell did you two find me here?" Mayart said, disgruntled but resigned.

"Guarding you is our job," I replied, like I was explaining to a child. "We will follow you anywhere."

Mayart's lip curled. "Stubborn, aren't you."

"Giuseppe, are these friends of yours?" The girl who sat next to Mayart, her short strapless dress showing plenty of skin, raised her high-pitched voice as she looked from one of us to the other. "Good-looking folks. Oh, Giuseppe, you must really be a big shot, to have two hot bodies like this looking out for you."

Mayart scratched the side of his face, looking crestfallen. "You're here, and that can't be helped now, so sit down. Somewhere else."

I confirmed there was nothing out of place about the girls. Now we just had to keep an eye on any drinks brought to the table and anyone who talked to the girls. We had to stay close. A booth on the opposite side, at the end of a narrow passage, was open. One of the staff came after us, looking riled up since we were disturbing things, and we pretty much forced our way into the seats.

Mayart continued his muttering. I only heard a few comments, like "overeager," and "parasites," and other such pleasantries, but neither of us paid any mind. Instead we kept watch on our surroundings.

Two girls came to the table. They wore matching dresses of gold and silver, perhaps the bar's uniform. The outfits showed plenty of round breast and smooth thigh, and left so little to the imagination, it hardly seemed worth the effort to wear anything at all.

The girl with the larger chest introduced herself as

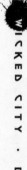

Sayuri and sat down next to me. I stood to let her pass to the inside of the booth. I needed to be sitting on the outside in case anything happened.

Sayuri happily pushed past me. "Oh, a real gentleman."

Makie's girl, who was called Machiko, did the same. Her long hair waved with each movement of her supple body. Before I could say anything, Sayuri called a waiter over and ordered beers and snacks. She took one of my hands and placed it firmly on her exposed thigh. Her skin was hot beneath my palm. "We can't let Machiko get ahead of us, can we?" Even without the invitation of the incitingly hot voice in my ear, my hand was already moving to explore the place where her thighs met.

"You're keener than you look!" Sayuri was surprised, but her tone soon changed to one of welcome pleasure. She wasn't wearing any panties, and my fingers quickly began the work of pleasuring her. Her face flushed, her mouth opening and nostrils flaring.

"Oh . . . that's . . . wonderful. Just your finger! . . . I've never felt . . . this before . . . so good . . . ooh, baby, yes . . ."

My fingers continued their careful, skilled work on her gently rocking crotch, giving her what must have indeed been a unique experience, even for someone in her line of work. Such finger work was a special technique of the Black Guard. If I were to take the male equivalent of Sayuri's job, within a week I would have every patron begging for my attentions.

Giving off moans of increasing intensity as she headed

for climax, Sayuri grabbed my hand and tried to push it deeper inside her. My finger gently moved against her clitoris again, making her entire body shudder. I stopped, and she ground her hips down, pushing my fingers against her clit.

"Please . . . please, let me come . . . please! . . ." If I were to ask her at that moment, she would tell me anything, from the amount in her bank account to how many men she had slept with. With a little more persuasion, a little more suggestion, I could have her kill others or even herself. Controlling women through sex was a common practice among organized crime and street gangs, but the techniques of the Black Guard were the next step up.

With a final finger stroke, Sayuri let out a long moan and passed out. It all took around thirty seconds, an average time for me. I checked to see how Makie was doing. Unlike Sayuri, Machiko had been silent the entire time. She was now breathing quickly but quietly. Her head was thrown back, her exposed white throat quivering. She was obviously at the height of ecstasy, but Makie had not touched her. The finger rubbing Machiko's crotch was her own, and it was her own hand that squeezed her ample chest, moving in slow, deliberate circles over one erect nipple.

Makie sat as she had been the entire time, paying no apparent attention at all to Machiko's condition. Every now and then she glanced in the girl's direction, and a strange light glowed in her eyes. It was obviously Makie causing Machiko's arousal. Each time she turned her face toward

the long-haired girl, her lips pursed a little, like she was blowing kisses. I was the only one who heard the slight sound of her breath, blowing on Machiko.

Certainly not normal breath. I didn't know if there were special particles mixed into the breath or not. The column of breath—so gentle, it risked petering out before touching its target—brushed Machiko's cheek and transmitted an indescribable pleasure to her entire body.

Makie's magic breath spread gently over Machiko's white skin, becoming a tongue, caressing and pleasuring her body in ways that no man could ever hope to rival. Makie watched the other woman's pleasure, and her eyes were so beautiful, yet utterly terrifying. An interesting battle, fingers versus tongue. Makie's lips pursed again, and Machiko slumped back against the sofa, unconscious.

"That takes care of that." Makie turned away from Machiko, seemingly indifferent to what had just occurred.

I nodded in agreement as Makie faced Mayart again. I sipped from my glass of beer. "I'll scan the customers who just came in. You check the food."

"Okay."

Nothing happened for a while. I extended the web of my senses, but didn't catch any demon presences in the area. Mayart seemed to have finally put us out of his mind, exploring the bodies of his companions. I had to admit that each time his withered hands disappeared beneath their skirts, or his thick lips sucked upon a nipple, the reactions of the girls suggested that he, too, possessed certain special abilities.

"Do you really think that's Giuseppe Mayart?" Makie finally asked. "I hate to say this, but I don't feel any unique spiritual powers from him at all."

"That may not be the best way to measure him." I chomped down on a cigarette. "I've heard it said that the more spiritually evolved one is, the closer to a pure human being they become. They get complete control over each and every human function. In other words, those who you can sense easily don't have any powers to write home about."

"I hope you're right."

I didn't reply, taking a long drag from my cigarette. Something else had caught my attention.

Something shifted in the atmosphere of the place. It was as though the air in the bar had frozen solid. The incessant background music started to cut out intermittently. I tilted my head, listening with more than just my ears.

It was happening. They were here.

I focused my entire awareness on the entrance. Ten customers were coming in—all together? No, in separate groups. I was too slow. In less than a thousandth of a second the enemy presence was gone. One of those ten was a demon.

The customers split into pairs, moving into different parts of the bar. Whoever was here with us was highly skilled. One of the big three, perhaps?

Makie, of course, had sensed the danger, too. "We were followed. After the spontaneous combustion in Ginza, they must have memorized our subconscious patterns."

I kept my eye on the new arrivals. "You know which one it is?"

"No, but he's strong. This is high-level possession."

That was why the presence had slipped away. The demon wasn't physically here; he had taken control of an individual's mind, not actually entering the body. In most cases of possession, the demon in control was off in some safe location, sleeping, operating their puppet by their will alone. Any precursors to activity would be signaled purely by the human being controlled, making it impossible to anticipate.

There was another problem. Killing the human to whom the demon was connected would take the demon out, too, in some cases, but we could not become murderers under any circumstances. Not only was it immoral, but with the odds of killing the attached demon less than 100 percent, we couldn't take the chance. The demons who could survive their puppet being killed were close to immortal. The only way they went down was if their body was entirely destroyed.

The only thing we had going for us was that human possession was a complex process. As long as we paid careful attention to everyone around us, there was almost no possibility of Mayart himself being possessed. There had been the potential for him to have been possessed between the hotel and here, while he was traipsing across Tokyo unattended, but once we started to worry about every little thing like that, we'd never stop.

Amid the whirl of smoke and ecstatic voices, sparks of

unseen violence were flowering. "A possessor could have sent their puppet in without giving himself away. Why didn't he just do that? Why the fireworks?"

Makie's voice was cold. "A diversion. To make us think there's only one of them, to focus our attention in one place. Possession takes a while, but I'm sure there are more of them out there."

"They know we're here?"

She nodded. I took another drag from my cigarette, organized my thoughts.

"They know what we're capable of. They'll come for us first. We can't allow another like at the Ginza to go off in here. I'll draw them out. You keep your watch over Mayart."

Makie glanced at me and nodded.

I stood, asked a waiter where the toilet was. Following his directions, I left the bar and entered the narrow corridor at the back of the room. There was a white door at the end, and the one I used to enter. No other exit.

I waited, cigarette still between my lips. The door to the bar opened, and a woman with short hair emerged. She was dressed in the same silver-and-gold dress as the other girls working there—an employee.

The door closed, and the girl smiled up at me with a charming round face. At least the demon had chosen a pretty one for his puppet. "No one will come in here for a while." It was the kind of thing a married woman said to the postman. Her sticky voice was filled with lust.

"When did you pick up our trail?" I took the

initiative—there was no reason to skirt the issue—and pushed back her attempts to entice me.

Her smile never wavered. "At the hotel in Hibiya. Tracing your subconscious patterns wasn't easy, but it looks like I made it in time. Mayart, you, and that betraying bitch are all going to die. Eventually. First you're going to join us on a little trip back to our world."

I took a long drag from my cigarette. "Sounds like fun. If you can pull it off."

"Trust me, I can. Now I want you to come . . . inside me."

Before she had finished speaking, her body split vertically. There was no blood; she hadn't ripped, exactly. It was more like a flower opening. Translucent threads hung between the left and right sides of the split, and a sweet, familiar smell filled my nostrils. The edges of the opening were slightly raised, like a pair of giant lips. A sticky fluid oozed from the pink flesh inside, and overwhelming desire grabbed me. My cock was hard before I could think. The woman had turned into female sex organs—a giant pussy. The juices moistened the lips and dripped onto the concrete floor. Aware of the male eyes upon her, the lips trembled with expectation and pleasure, starting to quiver as the inner walls rubbed together.

More than anything in the world, I wanted to go inside. I knew it was a trap, but primal urges beyond all reason made my entire body tremble. The desire to penetrate her with my entire body was overwhelming. Every pore screamed for release.

. . . Come to me.

The voice resonated in my head. Or rather, I felt the vibrations through my whole body. The lips moved gently, whispering again.

. . . Come inside me. What man would not wish it? Give in. I will take you, all of you, inside me and then let you sleep . . . so peacefully, sleep . . .

My feet moved forward of their own accord. The lure was impossibly primal, impossibly hard to resist. If I touched those lips, if I were enveloped by that warm flesh, I would spill everything, my whole being. Then I would be swallowed, becoming nothing but a slumbering babe, uncaring, even unaware, of the pains of the world.

I wanted it, wanted her, wanted to go inside. The impulse turned to complete and total desire, and my feet moved faster. I was close enough to see the trembling inner flesh, and the familiar musk of a woman's sex strengthened, paralyzing my brain.

My one remaining shred of reason cast out a final cry. I was about to be swallowed in darkness. Hot, wet, sweet darkness. Just before that voluptuous darkness swallowed me, my hand moved. It was an instinct far beyond my conscious control. My fingers touched the swollen flesh of the lips. They quivered, and the being gave a small moan of pleasure. A flicker of hope sparked in the corner of my foggy mind.

I had the training of a Black Guard. I could make any woman do my bidding with a few well-practiced gestures. But were my skilled digits enough to tame this monster? I

WICKED CITY • BLACK GUARD

turned my fingers to caressing the outer lips, and the pink of the clitoris was soon clearly visible. So she wasn't so different from a human woman.

Ohhhh . . . Aieehhhh . . . She still resisted, but the voice soon turned to one of enjoyment. My ten fingers moved tirelessly, giving ceaseless stimulation. The floor was soon covered with her slick juices, and the demon lost all ability to entice me.

It was time to finish the job. I moved to the clitoris.

Uhhhhhh . . .

The giant vagina moved like real lips, bending, quivering, begging . . . . *Don't stop, don't stop, keep going, make me come, I'm going to come. . . .*

Maybe that, too, was a trap. I stopped, flicking the fluid from my fingers onto the floor. I hesitantly extended my right hand again toward the clit. A series of white shards erupted from the raised edges of flesh around the opening.

They were teeth, almost as long as my index finger. The lips-turned-jaws slammed forcibly shut. Instinct moved my right hand away, just barely avoiding the snapping teeth and moving to my mouth. I took the cigarette stub, still between my lips, and jammed it into the flesh.

The instant the tiny flame of my cigarette touched the moist flesh, it exploded in a blinding flash.

"Ughhhh! . . ." The demon screamed. The teeth gnashed, sparks flew.

My consciousness, sealed away to block my enemy's attack, returned. Hypnotism, mind control—they could not affect me. My body's reactions were faster than my brain. By the time I actually smelled the burning meat, I had already jumped three meters backwards and drawn my gun.

I fired one-handed. My arm was thrown backwards, the recoil from a shot that could shatter two concrete blocks at fifteen meters pounding into my shoulder. It was as though an orange line had been drawn from the barrel of my gun. The .44 caliber silver tip made a glittering arch, like a tracer bullet, before it vanished into the burning, smoking mass of female flesh. Two wounds—one entrance, one exit—the size of an adult's head appeared almost simultaneously. The demon's scream ricocheted in the tight space of the corridor.

I dashed to the door as the corpse fell to the ground. I shoved my right hand, along with the gun, into my jacket. The woman's body was already liquefying at my feet. She hadn't been just a simple puppet. This was more than simple mind control—the entire composition of her body had been altered.

Rage seethed in my belly for a moment, but I soon brought it under control. Rage I could handle, but the sheer pointlessness of her death was another matter. It had been a messy death, anyway. Hopefully the puppet master had died along with his puppet.

I opened the door to the bar and looked out. The vocalist had changed, but everything else was exactly the same as before. A number of people stood, almost simultaneously, as if they had just remembered they needed the toilet.

When I had first confronted her, the puppet said no one would disturb us. She had soundproofed the corridor somehow. My gunshot blast had probably not made it to this side, either, then.

I waited for the people to pass, just to be sure there were no more demons or puppets among them, and then hurried back to my seat. Everything seemed normal, until I reached our seats. Our booth and Mayart's were the only ones enveloped in an aura of foreboding.

Mayart stood, suddenly pale. The girls looked at each other, obviously wondering what was going on. Makie was still calm, though, and that helped to soothe my own nerves.

"What's wrong with him?" I asked.

"He heard a shot." Makie's tone made it clear that she had, too. But had the girls?

"That's right, I heard it! A cannon roar! Your doings, I take it?" Mayart thrust a finger at me, voice filled with anger and fear.

"Please, not so loud," one of the girls said. "None of us heard anything. It doesn't look like anyone else did either. I think something's wrong with your hearing." Her expression said she wondered if something wasn't wrong with his mind as well.

"My hearing is fine, you cheap little slut." Mayart's Japanese vocabulary was certainly extensive. I was impressed.

The girls . . . not so much. "What? You rat-faced little

toad!" The stocky girl farthest from me shot from her seat. "Just say that again!"

Mayart paled, his tune changing quickly. "Ah, I apologize, I mean . . . very sorry, very sorry."

One of the other girls rolled her eyes at the tubby one. "Quit it, Junko, come on." The tubby girl sat, still glaring at Mayart, who was wiping the sweat from his forehead as he returned to his seat. She muttered that they should have let her hit him at least once.

Mayart lifted his beer. Something splashed on the surface, disturbing the smooth head of foam, just before it reached his lips.

"Don't drink that!" I jumped up, shouting—two big mistakes. For one, the glass had already reached his lips. And when I shouted, he reflexively swallowed a mouthful of beer. It poured past his lips and down his throat.

"What are you playing at, you idiot? Enough shouting!"

"Makie, get him outside and make him throw up, now!"

In an instant an elegant black shadow whisked the old man out of the booth and outside.

I scanned the ceiling. It was around five meters high, dotted was a couple of gaudy, cheap chandeliers. In one dark corner hung a small insectlike creature. My gaze still on the creature, my right hand reached out and grabbed a toothpick from a plate of cheese on the table. I threw it at the insect with the speed of a bullet.

The creature was skewered through the abdomen. Fluid spewed from the wound. The blood hit the booth

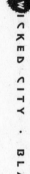

next to Mayart's, causing the imitation leather to go up in black smoke. Two girls dashed out, screaming.

The creature's body followed the fluid to the floor, the liquids turning to blue-black bubbles. The insect was the second assassin.

I stuck the M29 in my belt. I pulled some money from my wallet and shoved it between the tits of nearest girl before I sped out after Makie.

She had gone to the right just turning the corner as I was leaving the building. She had her arm around Mayart's waist and looked like she knew exactly where she was going. She must have checked out the surroundings before entering the bar.

I wondered why the old man wasn't putting up more of a fight, and then noticed that his feet were not touching the ground. She was carrying him. I smiled wryly and rushed after them.

There was no one else in the alley. The moon cast our shadows on the ground. I arrived just as Makie released her burden.

He finally unleashed his tongue. "What are you two fools playing at? You've ruined my big night out in Tokyo!"

"You made him throw up yet?" I asked Makie.

"I'm just about to."

"Throw up? What idiocy is this!" Mayart flailed his arms around, shouting. "I'm not going to let . . ." He stopped his squawking and grabbed his belly. An icy shiver ran down my spine.

Mayart's eyes rolled backwards, revealing yellowing whites. His body snapped forward, and the contents of his stomach splattered onto the ground. The stench of alcohol filled the narrow space. He doubled over, vomited again. This time he spat up a white snakelike creature.

A feeler hung from Mayart's mouth like a bizarre parody of his tongue, writhing in the dim light. The insect back in the bar wasn't the second assassin. This thing, invading Mayart's stomach when he swallowed his beer, was the second assassin.

Mayart's eyeballs fell to the ground with a popping sound, trailing their shredded optic nerves. The strange life-form, now wearing Mayart's skin, quickly came into view.

It took less than a second for four feelers to erupt from his ears and nostrils. Countless more feelers erupted from his shoulders, sides, and buttocks, tearing through his flesh and clothing. They glistened with a disgusting luster in the moonlight, perhaps from having absorbed all the nutrition in Mayart's system.

Makie supported the staggering body. The slimy tentacles wound around her black clothing and tightened.

"I'm fine. Stay back." Stopping me with a gesture, Makie placed her right hand on Mayart's chin. His jaw opened with a snap.

"What're you going to do?"

"Let me show you how we do things on the other side."

With one white hand, she gently pushed the feeler

protruding from Mayart's mouth aside. Her hand vanished into his throat, first the wrist, then the elbow of her black suit disappeared inside the old man's body.

Mayart's body quivered, and the tentacles dropped to the floor, slithering in an otherworldly fashion. When her arm stopped moving, I saw a little tension in Makie's face for the first time.

She didn't need my help. With a short, almost sexy breath, Makie pulled her arm out in one smooth motion. The tentacles were sucked back into Mayart's body, and Makie dragged a single thick white tentacle out through his mouth.

Her hand, covered in viscous white fluid, steaming in the night air, plunged into his mouth again to continue her grisly fishing expedition.

She pushed Mayart's jaw open even wider, and a large chunk of split flesh filled his mouth. Before it hit the ground, it opened like a water lily, four tentacles spreading outward, keeping it airborne.

The creature appeared to be almost weightless. It floated soundlessly, almost two meters above the ground, its white tentacles wavering in midair like a jellyfish riding the tide. There was no sign of eyes, nose, or mouth.

Makie's eyes flashed. The top of one of the tentacles was still in her hand.

The glint in her eye was the same as that of a batter when he spotted the perfect ball coming his way. Makie swung the creature hard against a nearby pillar like a baseball bat, moonlight glittering in her eyes. A sound like thick leather being beaten rang out, and glittering juices splashed all over the pillar and the ground.

Makie prepared to make another strike but was suddenly thrown off balance. She flew through the air in a graceful arch and slammed, shoulder first, into the concrete.

The demon had wound a free feeler around the pillar for support and then pushed Makie away.

"Makie!" I scooped up Mayart's eyeballs and dropped them into my pocket. The old man was a distance away. His body was full of holes, but his brain and heart appeared to be safe.

"I'm fine." Makie rolled her shoulders as she stood.

My gaze moved to something just above her. "Uh, Makie? Look out."

Right above her head, something white and bubble-like extended toward her, reaching for her. Unperturbed, Makie straightened her fingers and stabbed upward. She pierced the bubble, but it did not pop. Instead, it enveloped her. In an instant, Makie's body, from right shoulder to head, had been swallowed by the opaque spherical life-form.

Her bizarre attacker floated eerily above the ground. The side that faced the moon glittered as it drifted on the faintest of breezes. It had been created from the tentacle creature, which still had a feeler wrapped around the pillar.

I tucked Mayart's body under my arm and dashed for the entrance to the alley. I caught motion from the corner of my eye and knew the creature was following in my wake.

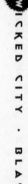

Halfway to the end of the alley, my vision misted over. Pain lanced through my brain like shards of glass, shattering my concentration. With much effort, I turned to see what was happening. A colorless protrusion extended from the exterior of the floating creature and had attached itself to me, burning my skin. The thought that emerged in my foggy brain was that it was some form of digestive action. The next thought: Where did the floating sac, which looked so delicate, store the ability for such functions?

I tried to peel the attacker off, and my fingers and hand were enveloped by it, rendering a pain so acute, it felt as though needles were being inserted into every cell of my body. My shirtsleeve melted like butter, button and material both.

The pain was so severe, I thought I might pass out. I pushed through the agony and focused my awareness on my hands, and turned my power toward the terrible thing that had grabbed me.

Its skin parted easily beneath my punch, pain replaced by the cool caress of fresh air. The creature sent more spherical attackers after me. In a few seconds, they were reduced to mush.

I checked to see that Mayart was still safe—if I could call it that—and looked back down the alleyway. Glittering beauty met my gaze in the form of Makie.

"It's gone." I looked toward the pillar, but there was no sign of anything suspicious. "One of the big three, you think? It was able to survive your attack." I checked that Mayart's eyeballs were still safe in my pocket and then pushed my senses into the surrounding area to check that the vicinity was clear. Everything seemed okay.

Makie picked some remaining shreds of the creature's skin from her clothing. "You're probably right. What now?" There were holes in the material of her jacket where the digestive creatures had eaten away at it, exposing her white undershirt and, in some spots, the naked skin beneath. The majority of the damage occurred from her neck to her shoulder, her elegant back and rounded shoulder blades exposed. I thought it was a welcome addition to her outfit. On the other hand, my own sleeve was in tatters, the shirt below damaged, making it look as though I had just pulled it off a beggar.

I looked at Mayart. His empty black eye sockets wept tears of blood, and his face was the color of ash. It looked as though he had aged fifty or sixty years in the last few minutes, a result of all that life force being drained.

"Get us a taxi." I lifted Mayart, supporting him with an arm around his shoulders. "So long as we cover his eyes, he can pass as a drunk. We need to get him to the hospital, right away."

"Pointless. His life force has been torn out from the very root. No human hospital can treat him now. He needs the highest grade of spiritual treatment."

"That's what we're going to get him."

It felt good to see a brief show of surprise on Makie's face. "Just get us a taxi, quickly. We need to get to Azabu."

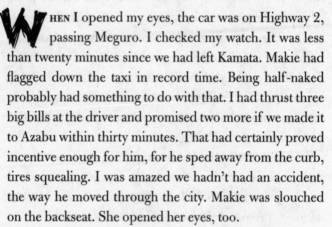

WHEN I opened my eyes, the car was on Highway 2, passing Meguro. I checked my watch. It was less than twenty minutes since we had left Kamata. Makie had flagged down the taxi in record time. Being half-naked probably had something to do with that. I had thrust three big bills at the driver and promised two more if we made it to Azabu within thirty minutes. That had certainly proved incentive enough for him, for he sped away from the curb, tires squealing. I was amazed we hadn't had an accident, the way he moved through the city. Makie was slouched on the backseat. She opened her eyes, too.

"You think we've avoided their trace?" I asked.

She nodded. "By inhibiting our consciousness for so long, it should be impossible for them to locate us, so long as they are not following us visually. The fact that they know we have been in Seclusion of Consciousness and haven't made a move proves that we have lost them."

I was satisfied with Makie's rationale. Since learning from the poor girl who had been turned into a giant vagina that we were being followed, it had been necessary for us to take immediate steps. As soon as we climbed into the taxi and confirmed that the driver was not compromised, we started the Seclusion of Consciousness. This involved consciously proceeding into the inner-consciousness, a level even deeper than the subconscious. It was a risky technique—one wrong step within that barren region led to a death that would have stumped even the most astute coroner. Our biological functions would have dropped to zero without any physical reason.

Even with the risks, it was nearly guaranteed that we would avoid the watchful eyes that had been so firmly fixed upon our subconscious activity. After all, someone who is aware of only nothingness is dead. Demons may be able to pick up on the fading patterns of a dead individual, but not those of someone who was essentially living-dead. That was outside of their abilities. A trace was impossible.

Makie's mysterious eyes met mine. "I didn't think a Black Guard from this side would be able to perform a successful Seclusion of Consciousness. I underestimated you. . . . My apologies."

"Don't worry about it. I didn't think you could do it, either. We've got bigger problems to worry about, anyway." I placed my hand against Mayart's forehead; the half-dead old man slumped against Makie's shoulder. I transmitted some of my Psychic Power to him, but the effects were minimal. We didn't have much time left.

"Driver. Take the Tengenji ramp." Even as I made the request, I wasn't sure I was doing the right thing.

Makie's eyebrows rose slightly. She looked as though she might say something, but instead just looked at me,

eyes as cold as always. She didn't need to tell me—I sensed it, too. The Tokyo night—the south Azabu night—was heavy with a premonition of death.

As we came off the Tengenji ramp, the lights of the Tokyo Tower became visible in the north-northeast. The driver's shoulders slumped, and he gave a heavy sigh.

"Is something the matter?" Makie asked the question, but her expression said she was well aware of the answer.

"Oh, it's nothing. . . ." The driver paused, but soon words spilled from his mouth like water, as though he had been waiting for this chance to get it off his chest. "I mean, I just got a terrible chill down my spine. . . . Did you feel it?"

We had, but it didn't affect us in the same way.

The driver continued. "I don't come to Azabu all that often, but I'd heard other drivers say that coming out here at this time of night always gives them the chills. I've been out here four, five times, and it's true. It's not a normal shiver, either. It's like my entire spine has . . . frozen solid, or something."

I looked at the darkness spreading outside the window and said nothing. I was concerned about Mayart's life force—it was so faint, it was almost extinguished—but there was something else I had to worry about as well. Nighttime in Azabu.

The walls of the French Embassy on Fourth loomed up out of the darkness. He turned left, and we passed the

Chinese Embassy, then the German Embassy. Finally our destination—the trees of the Arisugawanomiya Memorial Park—came into view beneath the moonlight.

"What's this . . . ," the driver muttered. The driver was much slower than me. I had already spotted the single taxi following us in the streetlight-illuminated night. It was a Nissan Gloria. The sign on the roof read TOKYO TRANSPORT.

The Gloria moved alongside our car, on the right, directly beside me.

"Nighttime in Azabu certainly is dangerous," Makie sang from the backseat.

The driver glanced into the car. His voice trembled. "Hold . . . hold on here. . . . There's no one in that car . . . !"

This was one of the famous sights of Azabu—a Ghost Taxi. According to various folklore and paranormal histories, Ghost Taxis began showing up in Tokyo just after the war, around the time taxis had begun to flourish in the city. Each account was similar—a car with no driver, appearing beside a moving automobile. It was said the drivers who saw these vacant taxis met with a nasty twist of fate, but I didn't know anything about that. Obviously many drivers took the story to heart—there were a lot of cabs with little mascots hanging from the rearview mirrors. Charms to ward evil, a tradition instigated since the Ghost Taxis had appeared.

I marveled at the idea of such superstition, but couldn't deny the seemingly empty car beside us. Were the streets

WICKED CITY · BLACK GUARD

of Azabu so thick with mystery that even Ghost Taxis roamed them freely?

Our driver braked, and the taxi slowed down, his slack expression one of abject fear. The other car proceeded to move in front of us. The Gloria did not appear to be threatening us; it disappeared.

In that instant, a feeling hit me that we had made a terrible mistake. I grabbed the driver by one shoulder. "Step on it . . . get past that car!"

The Gloria turned right, and the driver became more confused than before. "That's impossible. . . . There's not supposed to be a road there?!"

Makie's voice was on the verge of tears as she whispered, "Even the streets are on the move tonight."

I felt something like life force ripple away from her slender body. A phantom street suddenly appearing in the night was something that would happen in her world. Azabu was a place where our world brushed up against hers. That didn't bode well for us.

The driver looked to us for direction. "What should we do? I'd really like to get back to . . . normal streets."

"Not going to happen. This is the only street available to us now. Keep going." I was unsure what the driver sensed in Makie's voice, but he said nothing and returned both hands to the wheel.

"When did we enter the eldritch space?" I asked without removing my hand from Mayart's forehead.

"As soon as we came off the Tengenji ramp. It's because of me."

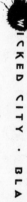

Makie's presence, because she belonged to the other side, had the ability to stimulate spiritual regions that were physically located close to our world.

I should have known better than to come this way. It would have been better to take the Iikura ramp and pass through old Azabu to reach the Memorial Park. But Mayart's condition was so severe that I had decided to risk it and pass directly through south Azabu. I had rolled the dice and lost.

Entering an eldritch space—a sealed pocket of eldritch power—was no mean feat, but getting out was ten times harder. An eldritch space was one of the easiest pitfalls for a Black Guard to fall into because of the specific type of Psychic Power—PP—that they possessed. An inexperienced Black Guard who did not yet fully understand how to control the natural power that seethed inside their bodies could unconsciously wander into an eldritch space and simply disappear. It wasn't easy to do, though, since the locations of most spaces had been carefully documented, and they "slept" during the day. Overall the risks were low. At night, however, when active, they added another layer of danger to Tokyo.

Many specters haunted this section of town. Drivers taking Aoyama Street in heavy rain sometimes bore witness to a red raincoated figure walking—or rather, swimming—toward Akasaka. Those few who paid the figure closer attention would notice the figure had no legs to support its smooth stride. A girl who met with a horrible traffic accident knocked on the doors of the shops near where she was killed, searching for something lost. No one opened the door in reply to her insistent knocking, because the residents of the region knew the truth of the girl's existence and about the touch of the other, separate world upon their own.

Hibiya Park, an oasis for the workingman during the daytime, was handed over to more eldritch residents at night. The giggling secretaries probably never see the small rusty stains by the fountain where they sit, taking a break to enjoy the hot sun, drinking cola. Only the park keeper knows the marks are actually bloodstains that he cannot remove no matter what he tries. Only he has noticed the tiny tracks hiding beneath the deep layer of dead leaves, and only he knows they are footprints.

The poor park keeper; his is a strange life. On the night of a full moon, patrolling the frozen grounds, he hears the apparent death throes of a wild dog. He squints into the darkness and sees a horde of slender figures attacking something with spears and axes that glitter in the moonlight. He's not surprised, really, not after everything he has seen, so he keeps to his fixed route, says nothing. Later, he will have to wash the blood away with water from the fountain and fetch the industrial bleach from the fence beside the keeper's office. He doesn't ask what happened to the flesh, the shattered bones. . . . He thinks perhaps they were carried to the underground kingdom of tiny people, its entrance a hole in a tree, or maybe into the branches of a tall evergreen. The man did not know that much. He is but one who knows his space is shared with a terrible type of

darkness that threatened humankind even in its huge cities of concrete, steel, and glass.

We continued down the eldritch avenue. A high stone fence was on our left, the concrete outer wall of a house on the right. It was a western-style building with a weathercock on the roof, and I couldn't help wondering for a moment exactly who lived there.

The Gloria turned left. We had to follow.

"We . . . we have a problem. No, two problems." The driver's surprisingly calm voice spoke volumes regarding the fear that gripped him. The yellow taillights ahead had doubled. "Where did he come from? There's no other way onto this street."

"Two cars," I muttered.

Makie's gaze was locked on to the rearview mirror. "More than that."

I looked behind us—a Toyota Crown tailed five or six meters behind. It was followed by a crowd of lights. A chill filled my stomach. We weren't going to get out of here easily. The space itself didn't appear to be threatening us, but those who lived here were unlikely to be so benign. I turned to Makie.

"What are the properties of this particular eldritch space?"

"Enclosure ratio . . . one to seven billion parts shade. It also has a high compatibility rate with human reality. We can break through."

"You sure?"

Makie nodded. "There's no way to tell where we will be kicked out, though."

I rubbed my forehead. We would be all right if we ended up inside the city, but if we ended up at the North Pole or out at sea, it would be game over. The way these eldritch spaces could bend space, and their penchant for trickery, was beyond the imagining of humans.

We had to do something. "Let's start by looking for a weak spot."

Mayart's breathing was so shallow that for a moment I thought it had stopped, and a desperate need to act crept across me. If my memory served me correctly, then the eldritch space in south Azabu . . .

"Hold on, before you do anything." Makie pointed a tool—part metal, part crystal—toward the car window. There was an odd but thrilling pulse, and for a moment it seemed time had stopped.

"South," Makie said abruptly.

"Yeah, that's all well and good," I replied. "But that's going to take us through a nasty area. According to the three-dimensional map created by the Tokyo team, the worst dregs of entire region hang out in the south."

"That can't be helped. Mr. Driver, I'm going to need you to follow my directions exactly, okay?"

He sounded desperate but determined. "I don't see that I have any choice, do I?"

His determination wasn't enough, though. Before Makie could give the driver a single direction, a fleet of driverless

WICKED CITY · BLACK GUARD

taxis surrounded our car, giving us no choice but to be swept along with them. Each passing second brought Mayart closer to the gates of complete and final death, but there was no break in the river of cars.

Just as I had decided to risk stopping the cab, the stone walls enclosing us ended. An open space appeared in front of us. It was barricaded so that we were funneled into the space. All the cars headed into it.

"What should we do?" the driver asked.

I shrugged. "What can we do? Go with the flow. Maybe this is where they rest up?"

That was exactly what it was. The driverless cars, perhaps after another night of cutting through city streets and scaring the population entered a wide empty lot. When the cars reached a corner of the lot, their engines were suddenly cut short, their lights vanished.

This was their lair.

The driver seemed to have found a measure of calm. "What should I do now?"

I gave the driver a reassuring pat on the shoulder. "They don't seem to consider us a threat. Maybe they haven't even noticed us. When the final one comes in, make a break for it."

"They won't come after us?"

"Not sure. Do you think you can lose them?"

"Hah! Of course I can lose them!" Passion ignited in the driver's voice; an unexpected but pleasant result. "We drivers aren't the type to back down. I've driven from

Tokyo to Atami doing eighty all the way. I'm not gonna lose to a bunch of drivers who aren't even there!"

A white hand brushed his cheek, and I caught a whiff of Makie's scent. "Do your best. You'll make it."

"Leave it to me!" He suddenly sounded possessed, on fire. Just a few words of encouragement from Makie, and he was a changed man. That was the magic of a woman from the other side, a type of feat someone from our world could never replicate. She left the driver to his own devices and faced me. "So? How is he?"

"Bad. His biorhythm is almost flat-lining. He won't last another thirty minutes. Even if we go sixty, it's going to be twenty minutes to the south edge of the eldritch space, and another ten to the hospital, if we're lucky. It's gonna be tight."

"Then we need to do something." I heard emotion in Makie's voice for the first time. "If this is the real Mayart, and his death leads to a breakdown of the Treaty signing, it may make future treaties impossible. The Militants will invade in force."

I knew exactly what that would mean for our world. Everyone would learn about the other side. It would start nearby. Those alleyways that gave people the shivers would become deathtraps, dragging people away by the dozen. People would blame a hungry pack of wild dogs, or a wild beast escaped from a nearby zoo. Before long, the number of such incidents on a national level would reach a point that the authorities could not ignore.

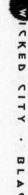

They would realize that something was terribly wrong. Something unknown was eating people. Before long, the attacks would spread outward from the center, like a plague. And like during the Black Plague, people would lose the will to live. They would revert to baser animals, becoming raging beasts of violence, killing and raping as they pleased. A darkness that no one could see and that none could stop would spread, expanding without end, mixing with and welling up from other points, eventually covering the entire island of Japan in clouds of darkness.

Before it got that far, the government would already have become aware that this bizarre and terrible series of circumstances was not limited to Japan, but was occurring across the entire world.

Of course, we would do our very best to resist them. Spiritualists, holy men, monks—everyone who can command PP would rise up and join the final battle. But when it came to sheer numbers, our warriors couldn't hold a candle to the hordes from the other side. According to calculations made by the Statistics Division, one in five thousand people had enough PP to even think about taking them on. World population being about five billion meant an army of around a million. That number included those with subconscious abilities of which they were not yet aware. An optimistic estimate said maybe only 10 percent of that number actually had the skills to take part in a battle for life and death. Maybe ninety thousand people would be all the defense humankind would have to prevent an all-out war between the two worlds.

We would also have the Black Guard from their side, but if the Treaty were to lose its power, then they, too, would return to being residents of the other side. How many of them would still be able to place the social order of our world above the logic and brutal philosophy of their own? How much blood, both demonic and Black Guard, would be spilled while the top brass on both sides tried to hammer out their differences?

"There's the last car," Makie said.

A gray Toyota Corolla passed through the entrance, the tail end of the procession of cars. It was now or never.

When the vibrations of the Corolla's passing ceased and its lights disappeared, I tapped the driver on the shoulder.

"Take it quietly. Let's try not to get noticed."

"How'll we know?"

"I will. She will, too."

Perhaps realizing that any further questions were pointless, the driver tightened his shoulders and shifted the car into gear. The lot started to slip behind us slowly. I regulated my breathing and started to circulate PP through my entire body. The PP flowed from the center of my body and spread to my hands, lungs, and abdomen, passing down my legs to the tips of my toes. Within two seconds, every cell in my body was charged with spiritual vigor. It was an immutable energy that supported life, different from the concept of physical stamina. The energy I used back in the alleyway outside the bar had already been recovered.

I drew my M29 from the shoulder holster with my right hand. Makie slid her hand inside her jacket.

The driver said nothing. He wasn't checking the rearview mirror, either. Every nerve of his body was focused on driving as silently as possible. Sweat beaded on the back of his neck. Even the muffled engine sounded nervous, on edge.

The driverless taxis did not move. Mayart's life force, pulsing through his forehead to the palm of my left hand was practically zero.

We passed between the rows of taxis and turned left. The exit was twenty meters ahead. The rank-and-file of taxis filled the lot, but let us pass without moving.

Seven meters. Almost there.

Five meters. It looked like we would make it.

Three meters . . .

A flash dazzled our eyes through the left-side window. The sounds of engines revving up surrounded us.

DREAMWORLD HOSPITAL

PART FOUR

J

THE DRIVER'S calm snapped like a piano wire pulled too tight. "They're on to us!" Our engine roared to life like the taxis that surrounded us. The driver stomped the accelerator, and sudden speed pressed us back in our seats. The driver gave a whoop as he floored it.

The driver's confidence had been more than bluster. We tore past the row of rapidly lighting-up cars and turned right without losing speed. The cab was practically on two wheels as we made a daredevil exit from the lot.

The rear window was a cluster of sparkling lights. The Ghost Taxis divided into smaller squads and gave chase.

The driver smacked the steering wheel in triumph. "Which way?"

Makie pointed. "Turn left, right there!"

I let Makie handle the directions and with one hand pointed my M29 into the rear window. I lined up my shot, but wasn't about to make the first move, not until we knew what the Ghost Taxis intended for us.

Statistics Division had never reported an incident of a Ghost Taxi attacking anyone. We were apparently the first.

The roar of the engines sounded like thunder. A Nissan Skyline raced up behind us and, without any hesitation, slammed into the rear end. Only the driver reacted, grunting in surprise. Makie retained her perfect composure.

I shouted to Makie, "Watch Mayart!" and smashed the window glass with the butt of my M29. I stuck my gun through the open window in an attempt to warn the Skyline off, but it rammed us again. Our car slammed to the right side of the road, and I almost put my head through the broken glass.

City streets appeared on both sides. I caught a glimpse of a shop, shutters closed, with a vending machine that offered reading material similar to the one we had vandalized earlier that night. I briefly wondered who around here used it.

The Skyline fell back a little and then started to close in again. I aimed and pulled the M29's trigger. The gun jerked upward and hit the top of the window, sending out a shower of pulverized glass. A huge hole opened in the

Skyline's hood, as though it had been hit by antitank cannon fire. The front of the car bounced upward.

I had pierced the engine, as planned. Compressed gasoline spewed from the hood, the pistons tore apart, and the Skyline quickly lost speed.

It may be the highest-powered handgun in the world, but that kind of damage didn't come from any old .44 Magnum. My gun was infused with PP for Black Guard use, greatly boosting the physical destructive power of the weapon. Being in an eldritch space may have helped magnify it a bit, too.

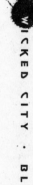

The sound of several dull impacts resonated from the dark road behind us. The cars that followed the Skyline hadn't been able to avoid the wreckage. They were going so fast, they collided with the remains of the first cab, at least one going up in flames. No further pursuers appeared.

Makie glanced back, holding Mayart with one well-muscled arm. "Think they've given up?"

"We can't be sure, yet," I replied, still looking behind us. "They may take other streets, try to cut us off. How close are we?"

"Less than ten minutes, if we can keep this speed up."

A glimmer of hope loosened the tension around my heart. "Looks like we'll make it."

The car rolled through the dark streets without further incident. Soon a darkly inked shop sign appeared in front of us. We passed a shop window lined with bright dresses and accessories. Lights from a police substation glowed in the night. We were on the edge of the eldritch space. But something was still wrong. There was not another single car on the street with us.

After we had gone a little farther, Makie told the driver to stop. "We've arrived. Let's get out. You, too."

"And do what?" The driver sounded sure we were about to abandon him.

"We can't take the car where we're going. No arguments. We'll compensate you for it later."

The driver's face paled in the glow of a streetlight. "J-Just who are you people?"

I sighed. "Today I hardly know the answer myself."

"No, then, the answer is no! I'm not leaving my car!"

I didn't want to, but the driver left me no choice. I thrust the barrel of my .44 Magnum against the nose of the poor man who didn't want to leave his beloved taxi behind, and forced him out of the vehicle, carrying Mayart along with me. It was summer, and should have been the hottest part of the night, but a strange coolness prickled across my skin.

A large bank loomed in front of us, shutters closed. The sign on the wall read FIRST INDUSTRIAL BANK—UPPER AZABU BRANCH. We were in Upper Azabu.

Makie climbed the stone steps that led to the building and took out the same tool she had used in the car. She placed it against the bottom of the shutter and turned it on. Apparently it was a tool for opening a hole in the eldritch space. So the demons, far more sensitive to eldritch spaces than we are, had developed a way to get out of them sooner than we had.

The driver looked around nervously. "Where . . . where are we now? How are you going to get me back to Kamata?"

I turned to the protesting driver, but my reply was cut short. A violent explosion vibrated the ground beneath our feet.

The taxis had caught up with us. I pushed the driver toward the bank and started to follow. I had gone only a few steps when something pinched my cheek. At the same time, the driver gave a yelp and grabbed his own face. I knew right away what was going on. The space was twisting. Makie's toy was finally starting to do its job. The relief at finally leaving this nightmare more than made up for the pain.

The driver stopped his yelling, his jaw slack and eyes wide. I followed his awestruck gaze. In the space in front of Makie, a large semi-opaque crease—in the space itself—rolled outward.

It vanished in the blink of an eye. Just when I thought Makie had messed up, it appeared again. Another crease, created by the twisting of a three-dimensional space.

Makie headed toward it. "Watch out. Touch it, and you'll be torn apart. Quick, this way!"

I managed to successfully guide the driver, his eyes now glazed, to the stone steps. I was just about to follow when something hammered into my back. I looked around, just in time to see the driver's beloved car slammed across

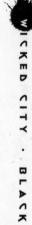

the street and wrapped around the streetlight on the other side.

Another shock wave washed over me, almost knocking me off my feet. The culprit was a Toyota Corona Mark II. Its bumper was bent inward and lights shattered, but that didn't stop it from reversing in a screech of tires and smoking rubber. It changed direction to face the steps and raced toward us.

I thought it would simply crash into the bottom step, but at the last moment, its lights fixed upon me, and without losing any speed, it started up the steps.

Even though it was moving fast, there was plenty of time for me to fix my sights upon it. With a roar and flash of light, a huge hole bored into the nose of the Mark II. The force of the blast shunted the car backwards, exposing its unprotected belly.

I pulled the trigger again, and my .44 Magnum roared a second time. With a satisfying thunk, the car took the full force of the shot and tumbled away. It dropped back onto the street with a metallic crunch.

Makie shouted from the top of the steps. "I've got an exit!"

I grabbed the driver, who had slumped down on the steps, and dragged him to the top.

"I've made a hole, but can maintain it for only ten seconds. Once you see the other side, jump through."

The driver's knees shook. "But . . . but . . ."

"Don't worry. . . . I'll have my hand on your back," I assured him.

An ominous sound heralded the arrival of three more taxis on the street below. They churned out exhaust as they plowed toward us. I had no idea how they had located us, but their noses twisted toward us and they raced in our direction.

"Now!"

Makie's shout made me turn away from the attacking taxis. A three-meter-high, one-meter-wide elliptical hole had opened in front of us. Not in the wall, but in space itself. As soon as I saw the familiar south Azabu scenery on the other side, I gave the driver a hearty shove on the back.

He stumbled through headfirst, his surprised shout vanishing as quickly as he did.

Makie yelled over the scream of the oncoming cars. "I need to control the device. You go next!"

"Come with me!"

"I can't."

"Come on!" I grabbed her black-suited arm and pulled her toward me, just as one of the cars hit the bottom of the steps and leaped upward like a giant killer fish breaking free of the spray. The second and third cars were just behind it.

The rift in space was closing in front of my eyes. Just before it sealed completely, I witnessed an incredible sight. Three cars, flying through the air, got caught in the spatial crease and were twisted in two.

2

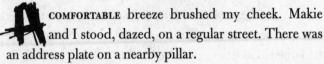

A COMFORTABLE breeze brushed my cheek. Makie and I stood, dazed, on a regular street. There was an address plate on a nearby pillar.

Makie pointed to it. "Look, we're still in south Azabu. We made it, then."

I placed Mayart on the ground and, while still transferring PP to him, nodded to Makie as she searched the area. I held my M29 underneath my jacket.

"We did." It took only a second for me to understand what she meant. "So what happened to the driver?"

She shrugged. "I don't know. Our Psy Power fixed our own coordinates, but he could have been kicked out anywhere. I just hope he ends up somewhere they understand Japanese."

It was a cold remark. I felt my first pang of dislike for Makie. But there was no time to worry about it now. I was too tired.

"Very well. Our first priority is getting Mayart to the hospital. Let's go."

"Another taxi?" Makie looked around, as if searching for one.

"We can walk. It's less than five minutes from here. But we need to move, because, you know . . ."

(vertical, left margin) HIDEYUKI KIKUCHI

Makie nodded—she knew. The PP she had used in order to tear through the eldritch space would have been sensed by the demons. We needed to avoid risking further causalities.

I threw Mayart over my shoulder, and we hurried through the empty streets. A look at the clock on the front of a bank said it was eight o'clock. Two hours had passed since we got into the taxi. Time passed very slowly inside an eldritch space. A second of normal time would be six minutes within the darkness of an eldritch space.

As the trees of Memorial Park came into view under the moonlight, an unexpected warm breeze washed over my entire body. My hand tightened on the grip of my M29. But my fingers soon loosened. I did not sense a demonic presence. It was more vivid, and yet obviously did not fit into our world. It was something on our side, not of the demonic realm. That could mean only one thing.

"You know what this is?"

The tone of Makie's voice made me turn around and look at her. "What's wrong? Are you . . . shaking?"

"A little," the trembling black silhouette admitted. "The smell and eldritch energy in this wind . . . it's not really my thing."

"So you do have some weaknesses."

"Happy to hear that?"

"Yeah."

Makie smiled. It was the first truly human expression I had seen on her face.

I moved close to her. "Don't worry. I've got your back.

Close your eyes, if you need to. You can hold on to my jacket."

"You're too kind."

She took hold of my sleeve. Now I liked her. The power-rich wind seemed to originate farther down the street. I wanted to avoid a face-to-face confrontation if possible, but there was no other route.

Makie's trembling was transmitted to me through my sleeve. I used my free hand to touch Makie's arm. She was my partner, after all.

A small pyramid-shaped object came into view, sitting by the side of the road. My suspicions were confirmed. I could hardly believe it—here, now, of all the times and places . . . I bit my lip.

A strange noise rang out from within the pyramid. I couldn't identify it, but if forced to describe it, I would say it sounded like the snore of a bull. Just like the reports had said. I smoothed the front of my jacket.

"It's sleeping. Just try to pass by as quietly as possible," I whispered.

Makie nodded—at least, I thought she did.

We proceeded without talking further. That *thing* shouldn't be here. This wasn't an eldritch space. During the day, this perfectly average street would be filled by the sounds of trains clattering past, the chatter of shoppers, and children playing. At night, it would remain normal and quiet. Yet here this thing was, sleeping. The street-lamp in front of it highlighted the blue-green pattern in its white artificial light.

We went closer, and I realized the snoring was coming from somewhere near the top of the pyramid. I concentrated on keeping my footsteps as quiet as possible as we drew level with the conical shape. It was on the far left of the sidewalk, nearly seven meters away. That gave us plenty of time to pass on the right.

The pyramid looked like it was constructed from a coil of thick rope—or rather, soft tubing. At least from what I could see of it; I could only watch out of the corner of my eye. Looking directly at it . . . would be bad.

The coil suddenly shifted in our direction. My blood hammered through my veins. The snoring had stopped. I wanted to turn to the side. To look at the pyramid.

It had already spotted us. Two shining eyes appeared at the top of the pyramid and were sizing us up.

"Don't look," I whispered to Makie. I left my M29 inside my jacket and used the hand to hold Makie's wrist.

There was almost no distance between us and it now, not even five meters.

Burning desire filled my head. I wanted to look at it. It was looking at us. Calling out to us, *Look at me.*

I shook my head. *I mustn't look. I must not . . .* My fingers tightened their grip on Makie.

She had stopped. I tugged on her hand, walked on, practically dragging her behind me.

Two more meters. I heard the sound of something slithering across the ground. It was moving closer. The eyes still watched us as it slid across the concrete.

I felt hot breath on my cheek. Makie leaned against me,

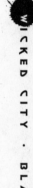

suddenly a leaden weight. She had passed out. She hadn't looked at it, only been overcome by its eldritch force. I shifted her weight so that I could drag her along with me as I walked, and we continued along. I still held Makie's hand, still pumped my Psychic Power into Mayart.

The creature was twenty centimeters directly to my left. Its breath was on me. And it whispered. Without speaking, it whispered, *Look at me.*

One more meter. A terrible desire to turn and look gripped me. It was similar to the desire to ejaculate, except that unlike having an orgasm, this desire sent ugly tremors through my entire body.

I wanted to look. Regardless of my conscious intentions—or perhaps obeying them—my body finally turned left.

I wanted to look.

But I didn't see it. My eyes fixed upon it, but my consciousness rejected the image.

So I kept walking. Just fifty centimeters more and I had made it. Makie's hand slipped from my own. Had she recovered consciousness? I looked over my shoulder for her, and fear lanced through my foggy brain!

Makie had not made it through yet!

I turned around fully, and there was Makie. She had lost all awareness of herself, and she was walking directly toward the creature. Straight into the gaping mouth of the giant snake.

3

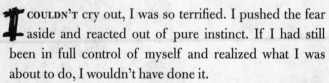

COULDN'T cry out, I was so terrified. I pushed the fear aside and reacted out of pure instinct. If I had still been in full control of myself and realized what I was about to do, I wouldn't have done it.

With Mayart still over my shoulder, I cocked the firing hammer with my right thumb and slid my right leg backwards to brace for the recoil. The weapon's beautiful chrome steel body reflected the moonlight like water running over its surface. I pointed at the face of the snake.

The roar of the shot shattered the peace of Azabu. A crimson flower bloomed in the snake's right eye. The red of flesh and blood.

The pyramid collapsed—unwound—without a sound. The snake's mottled body—so large, it filled the wide sidewalk—looked more surreal than frightening.

Blood speckled the moonlight, painting the stone walls on both sides purple. The impact of the snake's heavy body hitting the ground made it shake beneath our feet, but darkness swallowed the sounds of its thrashing. This was night in Azabu. This was Tokyo.

The spell on Makie had been broken, and now she stood rubbing her cheeks in confusion. I grabbed her hand and started to run. "This way! Come on!"

Behind us, I heard the sound of a window sash sliding open, a voice calling into the night. Someone investigating the gunshot.

Terrible power burned across my back. *You won't escape*, the pyramid creature said. *This crime shall not go unpunished. You shall not escape, never!*

At the end of the ditch, I turned right. The silhouettes of the trees of Memorial Park came into view, and the waves of the snake's psychic rage vanished.

The residents of Azabu knew the score. Deep in the bowels of the documentation section of the Azabu ward office, the Supplementary Ward History slept. Within it was every report into the bizarre and the strange that the people of Azabu witnessed. Included among them were many reports of the creature we had just encountered.

A particular monk named Gensho, centuries ago, wrote about a huge snake that was said to have made Azabu its home, snatching passersby both day and night before returning to its lair to digest and sleep. After the Shogunate fell and the Meiji era was ushered in, predecessors of the Black Guard learned of the snake's existence. Unbeknownst to those in the new Meiji government, these early warriors searched out and finally located the nest of the creature. By the time they found it, the snake had already moved on, leaving not a trace behind.

The snake Makie and I had just fought must have been a descendant of the one my own descendants had failed to kill. At a certain time of year, a certain time of day, many who lived in south Azabu vanished from the streets. They

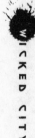

had seen the black shadow slithering outside their homes, heard the sound of its passing. Anyone who was still alive knew better than to go out after dark when the snake was about.

I ran west, along the line of trees, and the white walls of an institutional building appeared from the darkness. Hope filled my chest, and oblivious of everything else, I ran as fast as I could toward the gates.

It was my second time here. Everything looked normal. I dashed across the paving stones and was just about to tumble into the building's only entrance when Makie gave a shout and fell backwards.

I remembered, too late. Those from the other side were unable to enter here.

Makie picked herself up and sat on a rounded stone. "I'll be waiting here. Don't worry, go on."

"What if they come?"

"They won't break through those barriers easily. We'll deal with it when it happens. Mayart is our priority now."

She was right. I gripped Makie's shoulder. Surprisingly she was smiling as she laid her cold white hand over my own. The trip here had apparently brought us a little closer together.

I gave her shoulder another squeeze, hitched Mayart farther up onto my own shoulder, and entered the hospital. Inside was a wide waiting room. A white-coated man stood in front of a leather sofa. It was the Director of the hospital. I didn't know his name. Behind his round spectacles, a strange light glittered in his eyes.

"I'm Taki, from the electronics office. Personnel number . . ."

"I've been informed," the Director said with a nod. "Your boss sent word we were to look after you. We're on twenty-four-hour alert while Mayart is here in Japan."

He rubbed his forehead. A crew of hospital staff appeared behind him, including one orderly pushing a bed on wheels and a host of nurses and doctors. Impressive. The bed was rolled forward and an IV inserted in Mayart's arm.

I grabbed the nurse closest to me. "Wait, you'll need these." I reached into my pocket and handed her Mayart's eyeballs.

The old man was rolled from department to department, subjected to a battery of tests. After watching the full-body CT scan, I finally took up a place on one of the leather sofas while the nurses and doctors returned to the darkness of the corridors.

The Director came out to meet me and handed me a hot cup of fresh coffee, which was as good as life force in a cup.

"Foreign affairs is a tough gig, huh. No sleep for the Black Guard tonight. We've been getting plenty of reports of small conflicts already."

I lit up and took a long drag of my cigarette, holding the smoke in my lungs for a moment and then letting it out before asking the most important question.

"How is Mayart doing?"

"From what I have seen . . ." The Director appeared to

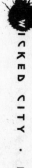

have left everything to his staff. "His life force has been drained by some demonic means, but your Psy Power had the desired effect. He'll pull through."

I pushed down the incredible exhaustion that washed over my body, but it still took all my effort just to nod. "How long will he take to recover, then?"

"Fifteen minutes, give or take." The Director blew two plumes of smoke from his nostrils. "Hard to believe this happened when you were guarding him, Taki. I guess they've wheeled out the big guns, huh?"

Noticing my surprised expression, he chuckled. "We're not without our own sources of information."

I asked the second most important question. "And this building is completely protected?"

"Spiritual coating is twenty times normal thickness. Most demons would melt with a single touch to the walls. There's a reason this place has survived five thousand years of demon conflict."

"Very well." I stamped out my cigarette in a nearby ashtray and stood. "I'll be back in fifteen minutes. Take care of him."

I didn't know exactly which generation of Elders had ordered the Hospital to be created. Even the Director, who had claimed five thousand years, couldn't be sure. At the beginning of the conflict with the demons, our leaders had quickly realized the need for spiritual healing techniques. The Black Guard were few and precious in number, and their wounds generally revolved around their Psychic Power. PP could boost the physical properties of flesh, so much so that a fully charged Black Guard could withstand the impact of numerous 45-millimeter rounds. This was little use against the spiritual attacks demons used.

In the beginning of our profession, many of the Black Guard were lost, not to the fangs of the enemy but to the life-sucking eldritch power that accompanied their bites. Those first pioneers, having only just formed the Black Guard organization, had been working out their own ways of using Psy Power to strengthen themselves. Bringing all these ideas together and working out the most effective way to bring forth such power proved to be one of the key issues of the time period.

The network of Hospitals, set up around the world, was the branch of our organization that had been created to re-search and develop these procedures. The requirements for a Hospital site were incredibly strict. The alignment of the stars, purity of the soil and air, and the history of the site dating back to the dawn of time were among the thousands of factors checked. It wasn't easy to find such a site, obviously. Sometimes it took more than five hundred years to locate one. There were only 257 in the entire world.

The healing methods and techniques created in the Hospitals became a vital lifeline to all injured Black Guard, and they were irreplaceable places of solace and healing. The staff and facilities were top secret, and there were few even among the highest level of the Black Guard who knew all their secrets.

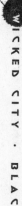

I headed outside and was taken by surprise. Makie was nowhere to be seen. Her powers should have been enough for her to remain on the grounds, even if she could not step inside. But she wasn't there.

Had she been captured by one of the big three, or a group of lesser demons?

Checking for enemy presence, I started toward the gates. A nurse called me back. Her reason for doing so was strange, considering the circumstances—I had a phone call.

I returned to the front desk and pressed the receiver to my ear.

"Good work—although you really messed up." It was Chairman. There was no background noise on the line, suggesting he was in the office.

"You can chew me out later. Makie has vanished."

Chairman didn't acknowledge the information. "They are throwing everything they have at us tonight," was all he said. "Two others have been badly hurt already. They'll be with you there soon. That's why I'm calling you. This involves Makie, too."

"What?"

Chairman fell silent for a moment. "Don't tell me you've fallen for her?"

I was surprised by the question, but not about my answer. "Not at all. What's going on?"

"We've found a suspicious corpse in Shibuya. A university student called Yazaki. His right arm was torn completely off, including the shoulder. When Takumura and his team gave chase, the demons made off with the arm only. They left the rest of the body behind."

"So . . . they intended to hide the body, even though they only wanted the arm?"

"That's right. They've taken an arm, so they'll be after legs and a head, too. That they're taking single parts only and concealing the rest of the body suggests they don't want us to know what they are up to."

"Reviving and controlling the dead—Victor Frankenstein all over again."

"Their creation will have some advantages that Victor's did not. The dead student had untapped Psychic Power that even he wasn't aware of. The demons are doing all sorts of nasty things behind the scenes, too, I'm sure. If every piece of their creature comes from a PP user, this could mean real trouble."

I needed a smoke. People with PP—the very power demons feared—had been injured and killed because they did not know how to use their abilities. Our medical facilities could create prosthetics that would return nearly all their functionality should they survive the attack, but we had still lost some of the people who should have become our companions. There were too few of them to lose even one.

Chairman sighed into the phone, blasting my ear with the sound. "Fairly large-scale conflicts are breaking out across the world. We've got our hands full. I can't afford to send you reinforcements. You'll just have to muddle through."

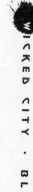

"Understood." Of course I understood. It left a bitter taste in my mouth, though.

"Luck be with you."

"Same to you, sir." As I replaced the receiver, a hand tapped me on the shoulder. A young doctor stood behind me, a pale-faced man of maybe twenty-five.

"Mayart is asking to see you."

I was still worried about what had happened to Makie, and the possibility of demons entering the compound, but the Hospital had its own guards. For now I had to see to Mayart.

I followed the young doctor farther into the Hospital. Small electric lamps provided the only light in the corridor. Doors to patient rooms loomed like phantoms in the dimness, lining the hall. Behind these closed doors, surgical techniques thousands of years old were even now being performed.

The doctor and I turned down a number of corridors before passing through a door marked SPIRITUAL HEALING CHAMBER. The room was bathed in waves of bluish light from powerful fluorescents. It was filled with electronic gizmos, all of which could be operated only by the touch of a PP user. Doctors and nurses lined the central operating table, but sticking out from one end was a familiar ratty face.

"You made it." It was a heartfelt statement, no sarcasm or irony in my voice.

"Thanks to you." *That* was sarcasm and irony.

"He needs only five more minutes' rest. Why don't you

stay here until it is time for the signing ceremony?" The Director's words were aimed at me, but Mayart was quick to reply.

"I'm not spending a minute longer than I have to in this stinking place. Once the ceremony is over, I'm going to the mountains of India. Tonight is my only chance to enjoy a little Tokyo nightlife. Get me out of here and into a bar, now!"

When the Director realized Mayart was serious, his shoulders slumped and he looked resigned.

I, on the other hand, wasn't ready to give in so easily. "While I would love to go with you, I'm afraid that won't be possible," I declared, as businesslike as possible. "The demons are serious tonight, more serious than I have ever seen them. Never have they been wilder before a Treaty signing. Didn't our encounter in the titty . . . my apologies, the bar in Kamata, teach you anything?"

Mayart shook his head. "Are you serious? That was nothing! I'd do the same every night if it meant getting my hands on some soft female flesh. Anyone who gets in my way—you, them, anyone—is my enemy!"

He spat out the words like venom, and I shook my head. This was not your average womanizer. Could this man truly be the real Giuseppe Mayart?

There was a loud slapping sound. Mayart ruefully held the back of his right hand in pain. I was forced to hold back a smile when I realized a nurse had rapped him on his hand for feeling up her ass.

"Oh, all right, fine. What about the woman, your partner? I want to sleep with her. If she's here, maybe I can make it through the night."

It was hardly the kind of conversation to be held in front of so many people. The Director gave a wry laugh. I think he was laughing at me. I sighed . . . and a faint earth tremor rocked the floor.

One of the doctors dashed to the intercom on the wall and spoke into it. Someone returned his call, and he turned back to us. "The demons are attacking. They are outside the grounds, using some sort of machine."

"Take care of Mayart."

The Director grabbed my shoulder. "Hold on, Taki. It's too dangerous to go outside now. Come upstairs with me." He ordered one of the doctors to look after Mayart, and left the treatment room, with me following close behind.

The quiet corridors felt different, as if the stone itself had knowledge of the events outside.

We took an elevator to the second floor. The doors opened, and we emerged into what appeared to be a control room. Countless computers, surveillance monitors, and other electronic equipment lined the walls.

A large semi-opaque sphere in the center of the room caught my eye. It looked a bit like a globe, but was misty inside, like it was filled with fog. Something writhed within, but I did not have time to examine it further.

The operator sitting in front of one of the computers turned toward us. "They're serious. It's a focused attack on a weak point in the spirit walls. They haven't used machinery like this since the attack on the Duomo di Milano in 1402."

"What exactly is happening out there?" the Director asked.

"An area five kilometers in diameter has been enveloped in an eldritch space. It's centered on this building. They're using a subconscious rewriting process to prevent the residents from realizing anything is happening."

"The demons still don't want to go public, then. Anything on the monitors?"

"Hold on a moment. I'll focus on them now."

It was not the operator who spoke—I thought the voice came from the strange globe. A moment later, the monitor screens misted over, cleared, and an image came into view.

The first thing we saw was a line of small flickering flames. They ringed a large piece of machinery. I couldn't tell what it was made from. It had two huge cylindrical poles, almost eight meters high each, like tree trunks turned upside down. A third beam sat atop them, horizontal to the ground. A circular hoop of the same material hung from the front of the crossbeam. On the back of the beam was a device that looked like a piston. It was poised to hammer a fourth beam forward, where it would pass through the center of the hoop.

With the dancing demon fires ringing the contraption, and the moon now out of sight behind thick black clouds, the device looked like inhuman rage made real as it sat there bathed in blue-green flames.

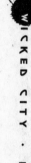

4

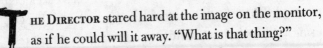 HE DIRECTOR stared hard at the image on the monitor, as if he could will it away. "What is that thing?"

The operator performed a few quick computer operations. "It's a Magic Wall Ram. There is record of it being used in the attack upon Duomo di Milano in 1402. It was incomplete at the time, so it couldn't do the job. It was destroyed by the Black Guard."

"Looks like they've perfected it." The Director's eyes glittered behind his thick glasses. "Increase the thickness of the barriers. Request aid from India and Tibet."

"It will take a while to open a communications channel through the eldritch space."

"Hold out until then. You've contacted Mount Takano, I take it?"

The operator nodded. "The Master and three of the highest-level monks have gone into prayer."

"This machine . . . what exactly does it do?" I asked. Vibrations were my answer.

Even as I asked the question, the bizarre glowing machine tilted to the left, right, up and down, like a radar antenna. It finally settled on a spot in the grounds. It had been shuddering with small vibrations, but stopped. The piston ratcheted back and smashed into the swinging

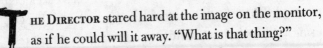

HIDEYUKI KIKUCHI

beam with incredible force. The beam flew forward and pierced the center of the ring in front of it. An almost invisible wave tore through the air, and the walls of the Hospital shook again.

"Evacuate the patients to the basement," the Director ordered into a nearby microphone.

I pointed to the monitor. "Is this going to be okay?"

"I'd like to say yes, but they aren't holding anything back. Use of that weapon is prohibited on their side, too. It causes too much damage to the surrounding area, and it has many nasty side effects. The Militants must have stolen it."

As though to emphasize the Director's words, the pole, which had swung back, passed through the hoop again. The screen turned white.

The operator's voice had an edge of panic. "A crack has appeared in the magic wall!"

"Holy crap," was all I could think to mutter. With each blow of the hammer against the magic walls protecting the Hospital, sparks flew, showering the ground with miniature stars. The sparks scattered, falling back onto the machine's supports and the ring, which started to burn crimson against the night sky.

Mist leaked from the globe in the center of the room. Our team wasn't beaten yet.

I headed for the door. "Demons may come through the crack in the wall. I'll go back to Mayart," I told the Director.

"Luck be with you." He sounded like Chairman for a

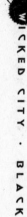

moment. I left the door swinging in my wake and ran to the elevator.

Mayart was in the basement-level shelter, clinging to his attending nurse and looking ready to shake himself to pieces. Each patient had their own room down here— aside from the two guards at the door and the nurse, there was no one else present.

Mayart began railing at me the second he saw my face. "Where have you been, you slouch? You're supposed to be my bodyguard, but you leave me all alone? Abandoning your duties, are you! I'm going to have your pay docked once this is all over."

"You've made a full recovery, I see." I gave the nurse with him a wink for good luck and went back toward the door.

"Where do you think you're going now?" Mayart roared.

"The guards here are suitably proficient. I'm going to wait for the demons outside."

"T-t-then leave the woman here. Makie, I want Makie!"

I stopped for half a step. "She's missing." The door closed behind me, cutting off Mayart's shouts. The building shook again. No matter how strong their weapon might be, and even if they did break through the outer spirit walls, those that surrounded the building were a different matter. As soon as India and Mount Takano were aware of the situation, they would send spiritual support. Our main problem now was any enemy that had already gotten inside the grounds.

I was sure their plan was to take Mayart out when he

left the building to go to the ceremony. That was why they had snatched Makie. I returned to the first floor, passed through the waiting room and out the front doors.

It was like midsummer outside. The demon's machine was covered in fire. The poles and pillars reached for the sky like hairs standing on end, blazing brightly, and the piston continued to hammer the swing arm, sending it again and again through the hoop.

I heard footsteps on both sides. I didn't need to turn around to know who it was. Three Hospital guards. "Are they inside?"

The man on the right nodded. "We were able to confirm at least three. They appear to be strong, too. Since their target is Mr. Mayart, I suspect there are more that we have been unable to sense as of yet. Either way, we are continuing the search." The man smacked his black metal nightstick into the palm of his other hand with a cracking sound.

The flames from the machine tinted everyone's faces red. It was amazing none of the sparks had fallen inside the grounds.

"Found them!" The shout came from my left, a little distance away—the parking lot. I realized they were shouting in our direction. I glanced to my right and left, suddenly realizing what had happened. *How could I have been so stupid?*

I gathered my Psy Power, pushed it down into my legs, and leaped into the air. As I flew, I drew my M29 in midair and looked back. The guard who had swung his nightstick

with such vigor was twisted like a dishrag. His head flew off. The body crashed onto the stones, convulsing massively then stopping. A tentacle emerged from the hole in his chest, feeling around for a moment before flopping to the ground.

As I landed, one of the remaining two dashed toward me, but the third stepped in and shoulder-tackled my potential attacker. I had at least one ally, then.

The two of them melded into a single shadow as they rolled across the stones, but the one who had saved me eventually gained the upper hand, pinning the demon beneath him and then bringing his special nightstick down with incredible force onto the head of the other.

With a nasty crunch, the victim's skull shattered into pieces, and the pinned man stopped moving. He smashed the nightstick down again twice before I reached his side.

The man stood, shoulders heaving. Although not equal to a Black Guard, the fellow still had a fair amount of spiritual ability. It made sense, for one guarding the Hospital.

He gave a little wave. "I'll check the parking lot."

"Wait," I ordered.

The man turned around. His thirty-something face suddenly turned fearful. His eyes almost popped from his head when he saw my .44 Magnum's barrel of death pointed at his face.

He held up both hands in surrender. "What . . . what are you doing?"

"Quite a skillful transformation," I said. I wasn't going to be caught off guard again.

"What do you mean? You saw what happened! I saved you!"

"Oh, I know." I nodded, pointing to the bloody corpse. "You can't fool my eyes that easily. During your tussle, you changed into him, and changed him into you. An impressive little trick, but it won't play to this audience."

Light flickered in the man's eyes, the kind that marked him as a powerful demon.

As he charged forward, my .44 Magnum blew his head apart.

It did not slow him down one bit. The same shoulder tackle that had saved me proceeded to send me flying. I flew back three meters, barely managing to land on my feet.

But the force of it had staggered my attacker as well. Both the physical and eldritch impact had been reflected by my Psy Power back onto the demon. Damage to the flesh did not mean as much as the PP energy damage.

I delivered a crunching right kick into the chest of the headless guard. My foot easily passed through his skin, punching through his back, and my leg was clamped down upon—trapped inside the demon's body.

Pain lanced from my leg to my brain. I felt my flesh tear. The demon was trying to get inside me! A highly unpleasant feeling sank into the flesh of my calf. It had been three years since I last experienced this sensation, while out in the field in Vladivostok. That time I had been bitten on the arm.

When a demon came into contact with a human, the

first thing they did was begin to alter him. Specifically, they started to change the physical composition of said human to make it easier for the demon to dwell within. Unneeded bones melted away, the functions of internal organs were rewritten, and the properties of muscles changed. Within seconds, the invading creature would acquire a new base of operations for itself, fitted to protect it far beyond its previous capabilities. If required, the demon could remain hidden within an unknowing individual for ten, even twenty years. But, if spiritual energy was applied to the human in question, or the demon's power faded for any other reason, the demon would be unable to break free, and once the human's life came to an end, he would be sent to the crematorium along with the body.

Even in modern times, stories about the cries from the cremation oven were still repeated frequently, and most of these incidents were grounded in demonic reality. The famous Haitian zombies, said to be living people rendered into a state of temporary death using drugs, were actually possessed corpses that had been buried, and then the trapped demon had crawled free. There had been a panic in Pittsburgh a few years ago when five of them had crawled from the same graveyard in one night. I was lucky enough to be visiting the New York branch at the time and had been dispatched to the scene, cleaning it up with the cooperation of the American Black Guard. We had managed to take care of the problem through liberal use of Psy

Power and flamethrowers, but a TV news crew caught wind of the story and ended up taping a few of the demon-controlled corpses. Everyone in our team suffered reduced pay for two months. I heard later the director of the news team was a man called G. A. Romero, who had gone on to create a series of genre-defining horror movies based upon his experience that night.

Anecdotes aside, I had just stuck my foot into the worst possible place. I gave up trying to pull my leg free and instead drew close to my captor. I stretched out the fingers on my left hand and then plunged them as hard as I could into the body's gaping red neck.

There were no bones. It was like sticking my hand into mud, and I reached all the way down to his lungs.

Just above the abdomen, I touched upon something writhing within the body, and I felt a sharp pain—the outer wall of its defenses. I focused my Psychic Power in my fingertips and then tightly closed my fist.

The demons defenses broke down, and I launched a full PP attack. The next second, blue-black liquid erupted from the gory hole of his severed neck. It shot three meters into the air, but rather than falling back down like water, the liquid clumped into a single sticky mass and hit the stone.

I heard footsteps behind me. The guards from the parking lot had finally arrived.

"Stay back!" I shouted. I aimed at the demon once more and pulled the trigger on my .44 Magnum. It was not

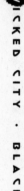

the bullet I was interested in, but the Psy Power with which it was infused. A hole was torn in the center of the body, and with its physical structure totally broken down, the demon ceased moving altogether.

The guards rushed over. I didn't sense a demon among them, but that didn't mean there wasn't one powerful enough to hide his presence from me. Even if they looked like allies, I couldn't trust appearances.

An image of moon-cold beauty flashed through my mind. *If only Makie were here.*

"You handled the others?" I asked the apparent leader of the guards, a big square man. His black clothing was torn and covered in green stains—badges of honor.

He nodded. "We took care of them. Two of our guys were injured, and have been sent in for treatment."

This seemed too easy. Maybe they hadn't sent one of the big three after all? No, that was impossible.

A creak and a crunch broke my train of thought. The fire that illuminated us quivered and shook, and the machine collapsed, swallowed by the flames. It looked like the spirit barriers received nothing more than a small crack, and even that was now closed. The extra prayer from Mount Takano or India must have been taking effect. So the demons' next move would be . . .

One of the guards let loose a wild, fearful cry. "What's that?"

Everyone turned in the direction the man was pointing. A terrible scene was projected into the sky, five or six meters above the main gate, like a horror movie. My mind reeled far beyond anything I had suffered moments ago. A bunch of street thugs dressed in cheap Hawaiian shirts were gang-raping a pale-skinned woman. Makie.

NIGHT TOUR

PART FIVE

1

THAT THE terrible scene was depicted a full ten meters across in the sky was surprise enough, but the content hammered me like a mallet to the head.

What had happened to Makie in the short time since I last saw her? And for her ravishers to be nothing more than thugs . . . The more I thought about it, the more rage boiled within me.

Three men pleasured themselves with Makie's body. One was making use of her mouth, another fondling her ample breasts, and a third had his face pressed between her legs. The man thrusting into her mouth was quickly overcome with pleasure and withdrew, ejaculating freely in the

air and onto her face. The man's Adam's apple swelled; then the skin on his throat split open, and a probing tongue emerged snakelike from the grotesque opening. A liquid the color of blood spewed from its tubelike tip, joining the man's ejaculate on Makie's trembling body. The slithering tongue then started to lick up the fluid.

I could only guess what side effects the fluid had. The fragile beauty who had until that point continued to resist and suppress the ministrations of the men started to visibly enjoy them more and more, and she stretched out her white arms and wrapped them around the man in front of her.

The snake-tongue, having completely covered her in its fluid, twined between her breasts before moving to lick her quivering face, then her lips. Makie turned her head away, but the tongue continued its pursuit, finally pushing those lips apart. The tongue proceeded to slide without hesitation into Makie's throat, becoming harder and thicker. Even as she choked, Makie was forced to suck it.

The man who had been fondling her breasts moved on, leaving her nipples taut and erect, glossy with his saliva. He started to kiss and bite her stomach. The one licking her pussy appeared to step up his technique. His head moved frantically between her thighs, and I couldn't help but wonder what tricks he was using—Makie's whole body quivered, her back arched, and she clamped down on the man with her powerful thighs as she climaxed.

The man kissing her stomach looked up. At some point, his mouth had split from ear to ear. White fangs glittered from this crimson half moon, and he suddenly bit Makie's stomach. Even as she shook with the pain of this attack, her body appeared to become even more heated with desire. With one hand, she rubbed her own blood all over her body. The blue blood from her stomach wound mixed with the sticky, crimson fluid, turning her elegant china skin into a mockery of filth.

The one forcing her to suck his bizarre member groaned, and his face twisted in pleasure. The fluid he pumped into her mouth spilled out and ran down her chin, neck, and onto her breasts. Semen.

The terrible mixture of blood, crimson fluid, and semen appeared to be causing a chemical reaction beyond the knowledge of human science. Black smoke curled around Makie's body, and she started to twist. I almost smelled burning flesh, and the guards covered their mouths.

The third, the one who had given Makie oral sex, changed position. He placed Makie's legs on his shoulders and penetrated her roughly. Even as he repeatedly thrust into her, the man turned toward the audience and laughed mockingly. Two red lights—eyes—glittered in the back of his gaping mouth.

This is what happens to traitors.

A voice rang inside my head. It was not young, old, male or female, but totally inhuman. The malice and evil confidence the speaker felt was plain.

This woman shall continue to satisfy my men for a while longer. She will be dealt with after that. How about making use of that time, Taki? I won't even suggest a trade for Mayart. Maybe you can save her. Leave the old man in the

Hospital, and I promise we won't try to touch him again. What do you say? Fancy coming to see us?

"Where should I go?" I asked inside my head. I had some telepathic powers, though minimal. For my mental message to get through, the other person needed to be a powerful receiver.

The eldritch space will open soon. Come to Shibuya once it does. The place is . . .

"Just because you tell me to, doesn't mean I will come," I interrupted coldly.

Oh, you will come. There are very few Black Guard in either of our worlds. I hardly think you can afford to just let this one die. The voice turned mocking. *Besides, this woman still thinks of you, and not with hatred. I don't know how you feel about that, of course. We'll be waiting for you. You have until eleven o'clock. That gives you less than an hour, but you should be able to make it. I know you'll make the right decision.*

The voice faded, and with it the brutal rape scene that had been projected into the sky.

One guard muttered bitterly, "Quite a show they put on."

That was enough to spark conversation in the rest of the men gathered.

"Now that was a fine piece of ass. I'd even fuck a demon if she looked that good."

"Why would they show it to us, though?"

"Why'd you think? If we surrender, they'll let us fuck her, too." The man who had said it started to laugh.

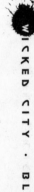

He wasn't laughing for long, not after I slammed my fist into his face. The feel of his nose breaking reverberated through my wrist, and the fellow collapsed to the ground, eyes rolled back in his head.

Sensing all eyes on me like lasers now, I turned around and headed back inside the Hospital.

Mayart was still safe underground.

I knocked on the door and then opened it without waiting for a reply. I got more than I bargained for—the back of a woman's head bobbing up and down beneath a blanket and a shout of surprise.

"You idiot! Wait until I tell you to enter!"

This was hardly the time to worry about the old man's feelings, however. I didn't look into the nurse's face as she wiped her mouth and ran from the room. "You've impressed me again, sir. I'm here to report that Makie has been captured and you're getting a blow job. Demons disguised as humans are enjoying her in carnal fashion even as we speak."

"Now that's something I'd like to see!" Eyes being the window to the soul, it was apparent the old goat was a lech to the core. Annoyed at his attitude, I decided to try to upset him a little.

"The enemy has asked that we trade you for her. Do you agree?"

"What the hell do you think, you worthless dog!" For a moment Mayart looked even more savage than the demons I had fought in the garden. "I'm . . . I'm . . . I'm Giuseppe Mayart! You expect to trade me for some demon bitch?

Unforgivable! Totally unforgivable! I'm going to report this. You'll be dismissed as soon as they hear my report!"

"In which case, you will be staying here. Although the Japanese branch has their hands full, meaning they can't afford to send anyone else."

He snorted a laugh. "As if you do anything for me, even when you are here!"

"Then we are in agreement. Please enjoy yourself. I didn't spend much time with you, but it has proved to be an interesting experience."

I gave a formal farewell, bowed, and then left. Dismissal, huh. That would make things easier for me, but it wasn't about to happen. The demons had declared their intention to kill me. I'd be tossing Mayart naked to the wolves if I was not around to protect him during the ceremony. In the end, I was going to have to stay here. A bitter feeling filled my chest.

An idea flashed through me like lightning. I dashed to the elevator and then on to the Director's office. It took twenty minutes to get what I needed.

Shibuya is built on a series of sharp slopes. They are so severe that some theorize it is the reason Shibuya has never been outed as the hub of entertainment in Tokyo. The location stipulated by the demons for my meeting was on a corner of the strip club haven near the Dotonburi Theater.

The line of love hotels was on my left as I passed along a street of drinking establishments. I turned left and came

unexpectedly to an empty plot of dirt and grass. Amazing to find a space like this in Shibuya, I mused. There were almost a thousand square meters cleared.

A shiver ran down my spine. The stunted grass was heavy with eldritch energy. Every blade of grass, the entire block of earth, was polluted with demonic energy. This was the kind of spot that even children avoided.

There was an abandoned two-story building at one corner of the lot, and a lonely wind whistled through the windows. The building was one of the top five most dangerous locations in the entire city. I would have voted to just wipe them all out, these demonic places, but one of the Treaty clauses, initiated one hundred years ago, prevented us from doing anything. The building had been constructed by a real estate company seven, eight years ago, but after a series of injuries and people falling ill, it was abandoned after just six months.

I quietly made my way inside. It was an empty husk, nothing but the concrete shell left. There was not a single door or pane of glass within. The only thing it contained was thick demonic presence.

Something moved around nearby. The vibrations in the air told me—I was surrounded by at least ten demons.

"I'm going to search you," one of them said. I did not reply, only stood still as human hands moved over my body. My gun was taken. That left me weaponless. I didn't really want to fight all of them here, but just as I getting ready for the attack, another one spoke.

"Straight ahead, down the stairs."

I did as I was instructed and walked forward. Three meters took me to a set of steps leading down. A pair of demons guarded each side of the stairwell.

At the bottom of the steps, I found a steel door. Light leaked from the gap between it and the wall.

I passed through the doorway without hesitation. The underground space on the other side reminded me of nothing so much as a chapel.

The cave, bored into the earth below the building, curved above me in an unusual way, the walls carved at a peculiar angle. Why the ascension rites favored by demons were conducted in places that appeared holy or religious to humans was still a topic of both contention and continuing research. The only illumination was a single naked bulb hanging from the ceiling. There was no sign of the tools or trappings demons generally favored in locations such as these.

The faint yellow light appeared to be in danger of suffocation by the darkness a few meters ahead of me. But what it did show me was enough to make me want to shatter that one small light.

Makie was still being raped.

The floor here was naked stone—there was not even a blanket. A different man from the one I had seen in the projection held her legs open and thrust into her. It took only a glance to see that this was not normal sex. She was lying on her back, and there was another man beneath her, thrusting upward into her ass. Double penetration. A third demon was forcing Makie to suck his cock. White fluid dripped down her throat and onto her breasts.

"So you've come . . . Taki."

The speaker was a shadow standing close to Makie's head. He spoke softly, and confidently, but with a combination of strong willpower and unremitting cruelty.

He stepped halfway into the light. He wore a light suit and tie, and looked like a man who could be my boss at the company. Nine or so thugs stood to his right, arranged in a semicircle for my benefit, watching Makie being raped. Not one of them even glanced in my direction.

The only sounds were Makie's sucking, the slick slurp of penetration, and the heavy breathing of men and one woman.

"This isn't the way we naturally have sex, of course," the suit said. "But having taken on the form of humans, one comes to appreciate such acts as the very height of pleasure. Young demons today are considered behind the times if they don't take on human form before fucking, or so I'm told. Please don't take that to mean that I myself am not fully aware of such pleasures."

"Enough dirty talk. Let Makie go."

"So long as Mayart remains inside the Hospital, time is your enemy, not ours. Of course, he'll have to come out sooner or later."

"I take it that means you have assassins in place. I thought we had got them all—how many did you send?"

"Oh, I don't remember," the man replied.

I glared at him angrily, but inside I felt relief. The demons, at least, seemed convinced the Mayart we had been guarding was the real deal. I was the one responsible for protecting him and hadn't been sure of it myself. But if the demons were willing to take the bait of one old man who may be an impostor, that was good enough for me.

The suit's light smile turned deadly serious. "So, why have you come?" He paused, perhaps to make sure this unexpected question had confused me, and laughed again.

"Then you still don't know what is really happening here. Listen carefully, then. Your duty is to protect Giuseppe Mayart. In his five hundred or more years of life, he has been the pivotal figure in maintaining peace between our world and yours. And yet you—and I don't know how you explained this to yourself—have simply left him behind to take me up on my challenge. Exactly why is that?"

"That's . . . ," I started to reply, and then surprise stopped me. Mayart was in a safe place, and the rescue of a Black Guard was a worthy cause. But without me, there was no one capable of protecting him when he left to go to the Treaty signing. If he was attacked during that time, the seemingly peaceful relationship between the two worlds would crumble, and both would fall into a hell of death and murder. I knew all of that, and yet here I was. I don't know why I hadn't considered it before.

The suit waved the question away. "No matter. You will

WICKED CITY · BLACK GUARD

understand soon enough. You are here, and that is what matters. The proverbial second bird, flying into the path of our single stone."

"I don't understand. What do you mean? You plan on killing us both anyway, I'm sure. The least you could do is explain all this!" Even as I stalled for time, I was carefully waiting for the opportunity for *me* to strike.

The three men clustered around Makie started to groan. They ejaculated. A moment after they moved away, the next three took their place.

"If the situation was looked at in a certain way, you have become even more important than Mr. Mayart," the suit said. "Let me ask you a question. . . . Watching Makie being raped, do you feel like taking a turn yourself?"

I didn't reply, not because I did not deem the question worthy of one, but rather I could not bring myself to voice it. He was right. My groin was enflamed with passion. Searing desire consumed my brain. A simple touch would make me come, and I desired to have sex with Makie down to the very depths of my being.

"You look unmoved." The suit's face hardened. "But I have my suspicions. You there, check him."

A female hand extended from the shadows to my right and grabbed my groin.

No! Time was up. My ruse would be discovered any second. I dashed from the shadows near the doorway and into the room.

The female demon checked what she thought was my crotch again. "He isn't hard at all!"

"Impossible!" The suit's expression changed. He looked at the woman, from her hand that had grabbed my crotch to other, in which she held the American-made pistol I had borrowed from the Hospital—a Colt .46 automatic.

2

THAT ISN'T his gun!"

His shout was my cue to act. I—the real me—tore through the darkness, heading straight for the first shadow I came across. I jabbed my fingers into the throats of all who turned to face me, keeping my body low, and then unleashed a low kick. My leg was infused with PP. To a demon, it would feel like the bite of a snake.

Knees snapped. One of the men's legs tore right off and flew off into the darkness. I punched through the incoming attackers on my left and right, arriving at Makie's side and taking her into my arms.

My raid caught the attention of everyone in the room. The other me, in an attempt to distract, dashed headfirst toward the man in the suit. His shocked look was only momentary. His lips twisted into an ugly smile.

Fear ordered my legs to stop, but I had to buy some time for myself. The suited man leaped into the air. Before my eyes could even trace his movement through the air, his knees came down on my shoulders. His hands laced together beneath my jaw, and he jerked my chin upward. The sound and feeling of my neck being ripped off made my body stiffen.

I saw the suited man jumping through the air with my head in his hands, and the back of my headless body as it dashed toward the spot where the suited man had been standing prior to his attack.

When the suit thought he was removing my head from my body, I was actually retreating into the back of the wide room, my arm around Makie's waist. There were still five, six of them left, but the .44 Magnum in my hand was more than enough to keep them at bay.

In the corner of my eye, I saw my headless body moving to attack the demon, now back on the ground.

My extended fingers headed for the midsection of the suit were easily caught, and with a shake of his hand, he tore my right arm from my shoulder.

Even he must have been surprised at how easy that was.

The headless me was not *me* at all.

I had gotten the idea from Mayart's rant about going over my head to get me dismissed, bolstered by my conversation with Chairman. With help from the Hospital Director, I had patched together some body parts from the Hospital and had a nervous system imprinted upon them. The headless me was nothing more than a copy of my real self, created using the medical advantages of the Hospital. My memory had also been copied and implanted in it, just in case. The real me had followed behind the copy to the building, and headed downstairs once the demons had lowered their guard. With them focused on the fake me, the real me was able to sneak into the chamber and save Makie.

With a nasty tearing sound, the suit plunged his hand into the copy's body. The shell crumpled to the floor in the face of the demon's mighty powers. A long sigh escaped its lips. It might've had only a short existence, but the double had more than done its job.

My eyes were fixed upon the corpse as it collapsed behind the approaching suit. *Out, out brief candle, thank you.*

The suit pushed his way through his minions, closing in. "Move. I'll deal with this."

So, the big three. The flying jelly thing we had seen in Kamata, another as of yet unseen . . . and this guy.

"Can you stand?" I asked Makie. She hung from my left shoulder. If we could take care of this one here, it would definitely make things easier down the line.

"I'm okay. . . . I can look after myself."

She sounded surer of herself than I expected. I nodded, let go of Makie, and gripped my M29. I relaxed my muscles, feeling loose, and started toward him.

Three meters separated us. A surprise attack from either side was impossible.

I faced the demon so full of PP that he had torn my copied body to shreds. The suit also had awesome physical strength. I knew those couldn't be the only abilities he had.

The man raised his arms to the side and bent his elbows, his hands in front of his chest. His suit ripped open

at the elbows, razor-sharp spearlike protrusions tearing through the fabric as if it were gossamer. The remaining demons in the chamber had formed a line on each side of the suit, three on one side and four on the other. The slender blades that extended from his elbows pierced the hearts of all of them. Their bodies jerked, and then they were still. The corpses hung from his weapons like bizarre sides of beef in a meatpacking plant.

They did not fall from the blades, but started to change instead. Tentacles and antennae broke through their flesh, emerging from mouths, ears, and anuses, and tearing through their chests. All of them, though I had thought them dead, quivered in pain. They were in the throes of death. Had the demon in the suit used his Psy Power to control them, or had they willingly lined up to meet their deaths?

I suppose I had some kind of answer soon. The suit's blades spun at a blurring speed. The skewered corpses flew off in random directions, sailing through the air and crashing into the floor, ceiling, and walls. Each body stuck where it landed, the sounds of flesh tearing and bones breaking ringing in my ears. It was as though their blood was glue, holding them to the surface. The suit smiled as the bodies started to swell and expand.

All this occurred in the two seconds since I had stepped out to face him. In the next instant I realized the bodies were sinking into walls. No, not sinking. It was more like assimilation. The mounds of flesh, hanging like strange pieces of art, melted into the concrete. The walls and ceiling, infused with what had been living flesh, started to . . . *breathe.* The suit had transformed the dead walls of the building into a terrible living creature!

Pillars, spheres, and other combinations of bizarre organs sprouted from the solid rock, hanging from the ceiling and bursting from the floor in all four directions.

It wasn't fear but rather surprise and curiosity that stayed my hand. Observing the powers of a demon in action was, for one of the Black Guard, not dissimilar to taking a long draft from a highly alcoholic beverage.

The entire space trembled with the creature's anger. Something ran along the inside of the floor, changing shape as it passed up the walls and along the ceiling.

A horrible realization gripped me. This was a *factory.* . . .

The protrusions around me split at the tips, and fluid of a color I couldn't identify erupted from them, aiming at the suit. Before it reached him, the liquid changed into a sticky goo, not unlike bubble gum. The gum wrapped itself around the suited figure.

Fixing my eyes on my target, I aimed one-handed and pulled the trigger. A massive bullet, capable of maiming a bear, blew a chunk out of the gunk-covered figure.

The man didn't even flinch. My trigger finger instinctively jerked again, the bullet screaming toward the target in an angry arch of fire and metal.

I couldn't tell if the Magnum rounds had been ineffective or if the protective coating saved him. For a moment, numerous fine cracks ran across the surface, suggesting success, but then the outer coat of slop, now hardened, blew

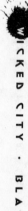

off his body like sand. From the middle of the whirling sandstorm, the suit smiled at me.

In the next instant, a .44 Magnum round, packed full of PP, tore from the barrel of my gun.

A small black hole opened beside his nose, then vanished. The sand reassembled itself around its master.

"You'll need more power than that, Taki." The suit showed me a smile unnervingly akin to that of Chairman. "This enhancement factory is tailored exclusively to my needs. You have no idea of the power it has bestowed upon me. So . . . let me show you!"

He leaped into the air. The blades, which had momentarily retracted into his elbows, extended again, this time toward my eyes.

I knocked Makie clear and wrenched myself away, barely managing to avoid the incoming attack.

As the suit landed, I smashed a left spinning kick into his midriff. I connected with the target. My leg shuddered, pain radiating from my foot to the rest of my body. The suit was completely unaffected.

The blades retracted and flew out once again. Sparks burst from the wall as the blade scraped stone. The suit brought it down before it reached the ceiling, heading right for me. It was fast. I moved, but was I fast enough to avoid the blade?

It closed in, sharp tip lancing toward me. It was going to pierce my heart. I had to move faster. Only twenty centimeters more. My heart was clear, but my stomach was in danger.

The lance pierced my abdomen. It pushed through, emerging on the other side, in my back. Cold exploded inside my body, numbing my brain. This was my first full-on contact with his power, and I found it to be far stronger than I had expected.

The other blade sliced through the air toward me, aiming for my neck. Perhaps the pain had sharpened my reflexes, because I caught the incoming blade with my left hand. Now I was literally holding the suit up in the air. PP leaking from my wounds, I spun my body as hard as I could.

The suit crashed into the wall, but the blades didn't budge. I grabbed my wound, groaning as I was tugged in a painful direction. The mud-suit shifted, guiding its master to the ground.

"Hah. I can dissipate the power you are feebly trying to hit me with. While the power I use against you . . . does this."

He raised the blades. My feet left the ground, and I was lifted clean into the air. I desperately tried to transmit my Psychic Power into him, but to no avail. With my wounds, I was weak. My power was about to burn out. The chill coming from the blades created a heavy pillar of ice behind my eyes. My nervous system and my muscles were frozen to the core, the heat draining from my body. I started to lose my grip on my Psy Power, to lose what feeling remained in my entire body. . . .

Vibrations and a terrible scream slapped me back into awareness. I focused on the scene in front of me. The walls,

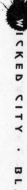

the ceiling, the floor, were all shaking. The scream had been unleashed by the suit.

A factory. Of course! When I tried to smash the suit into the wall, he escaped onto the floor. He could have smashed me into the ceiling but instead had simply held me in the air. Perhaps he did it to avoid damaging his precious equipment?

So who was attacking him now? Before I could even think, my right hand swung my M29 around. Desperation transformed the lump of metal into a mighty hammer. I broke the blade in my stomach about thirty centimeters down its length.

The demon cried out again, and hope stirred the final remnants of my PP. I grabbed the broken protrusion and pulled it out in a single motion. With it still covered in my blood, I rammed the thing into the floor as hard as I could.

It felt exactly the same as puncturing a demon's body. The organs that jutted from the walls and ceiling split, and the floor tore open, jellified matter spilling out like vital fluid. When it touched the floor and walls, they started to bubble and melt.

I swung my weapon again, slicing the floor open as though gutting a pig. Beneath the stone and fluid was a circular mass covered in swellings and tumors. Cogs and belts—or at least, organic-looking substitutes for them—moved within it. It was some kind of unit engine.

I swung the lance again, piercing it. The suit dashed toward me, but was thrown into the air when the machine beneath my feet was destroyed. His body and the factory were connected via some kind of fourth-dimensional superconnection. The same jellylike substance leaked from the suit's chest.

With the lance in one hand and M29 in the other, I dashed across the undulating ground. Halfway across, I jumped into the air and threw the lance downward as hard as I could.

The demon smashed it aside, but I had thrown it only in order to distract him. I took aim with my M29 and fired. I poured all my PP into the arching trail of flame that blasted from my weapon, headed straight for the suit.

His head exploded like a ripe melon. The destruction traveled down to his chest and lower abdomen. All that remained for him now was self-disintegration.

I made sure there was no chance for him to recover, and then dashed to Makie's side.

"Are you okay?"

"Pretty much." Makie smiled, her mouth still covered with filthy demon fluids.

I helped her to her feet. "A low point in the career of one of the greatest Black Guard from the other side, huh?"

"I should say so." Her expression said she didn't want to talk about it. There wasn't time anyway: the floor suddenly crumbled away. We dashed to the back of the room and up the stairs just before the floor completely collapsed.

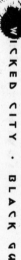

3

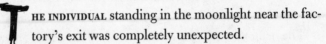

THE INDIVIDUAL standing in the moonlight near the factory's exit was completely unexpected.

"Mr. Mayart!" I was so surprised, I forgot the pain of my wounds.

Makie, leaning on my back, also sounded surprised. "What are you doing here?"

"As soon as you left, I put my guards to sleep and headed out after you." Mayart sounded particularly pleased with himself. "Then I contacted your boss and had him check for suspicious activity in high-risk locations that don't have an official entranceway. That's what brought me here. I wanted to find out what you were up to."

Perhaps my wounds were fogging my thoughts, because I couldn't wrap my head around what he was saying. "You put your guards to sleep? How did you do that? And what about the damage to the factory basement? . . . Was that? . . ."

"What are you talking about?" Mayart shook his head. "I only just arrived. It looks like you've taken care of things, too. Are you okay? Abdominal injury, is it?"

"I'm fine. Once my powers recover, I will heal right up. I'm glad you're here, anyway. Please, accompany us back to the Hospital."

"Not on your life!" Mayart easily jumped at least a meter into the air. He had also managed to put his guards to sleep—there was definitely something inhuman about him. Could the old man actually be the real deal?

I voiced my suspicions, as much to satisfy my own curiosity as to calm the old man down. "Why exactly did you come here?"

"Why do you think? To save you two! From the other side or no, she is a young, beautiful Black Guard. Her life is worth more than my own bones. I was ready to die for her!"

Something in his hand caught my eye. I clucked my tongue. "You should know better than to lie, at your age."

"What!"

"You're still clinging to that magazine. There are plenty of bars you'd love to visit just around the corner from here. So tell me again it was for our sakes you came here. I don't know how you put your guards to sleep, but I'm thinking what you really wanted was a little action . . . again."

"I should be so lucky." The old man turned to the side with a huff. "Whatever. But I'm not going back now. No way! If you really intend to drag me back there, then this is good-bye."

I looked at Makie. If he made a break for it now, I wasn't confident we'd be able to catch him. Makie had been brutalized, and my Psy Power was almost totally spent.

"Very well," I said to Mayart, who was already moving away from us. "We will take you wherever you like. However, you must promise not to leave our side again."

"Very well, very well." The old man's wrinkled face

broke into a smile. "There has been so much trouble tonight, to be honest, even having a pair of do-gooders like you nearby is better than nothing. We'll pick up some clothing for the woman and then take a Shibuya Night Tour, I think."

The "Night Tour" Mayart wanted to take was a late-night sightseeing bus that the transport authority had started the previous April. Some said it was a bold experiment, but its success was due to the bulk of the clientele during the hours of 10 P.M. to 5 A.M. being the playful youth of the city—the denizens of the night.

In reality, the whole thing was really a cunning trick by their elders. The "cool" sightseeing tour played to the young's inherent pride. Anyone who was anyone had taken the tour, and it helped the youth to reconnect with their city—Tokyo—instead of becoming apathetic about the city that surrounded them.

The whole thing was just another example of how, no matter the era, children are unable to defeat the cunning of their parents. In the three months since the tour had opened, the bus tours had carried more than 400,000 people around the city, more than 90 percent of them in their teens or twenties.

I purchased three regular tickets from the kiosk in front of the Shibuya Cultural Hall. Makie, Mayart, and I made it just in time for the next departure, which was midnight.

"I wouldn't have taken you for the sightseeing type," I

offered sarcastically to Mayart, who sat behind me. The seats were wide and spacious, lined up along the right side of the bus.

"Hah! You think I'm only interested in strip clubs and titty bars, do you? I'll have you know I intend to make my debut as an essayist in a few years. Seeing Tokyo at night is a vital piece of my research."

"An essayist?" Makie said. She wore the T-shirt and jeans we had purchased from an all-night store behind the station. While the masculine clothing concealed some of her beauty, the rough, casual style was still mysteriously appealing.

"Yes, that's right. Come on then, let's go! Driver—go, man, go!"

It was probably just a coincidence, but the engine rumbled into life and the bus rolled forward. In the next instant, we jerked to a stop again. The air compressors hissed and the door slid open. A middle-aged woman climbed aboard, dressed in a short-sleeved blouse. She was the last passenger, and now we started off for real, the bus 70 percent full.

The course we had chosen ran from Shibuya, along Aoyama, through west Azabu, Roppongi, Mamiana, and then into Shinbashi. The ticket was a fixed price, but passengers were free to disembark at any time. Most of the younger people would most likely get off in Azabu or Roppongi.

I cautiously searched among those on the bus for anyone with Psychic abilities, but there was no one. Going

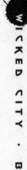

WICKED CITY · BLACK GUARD

through the procedure caused my abdomen to hurt, and I gave a little moan.

"Are you okay?" Makie asked. She sat behind me, beside Mayart.

"Oh, I'm fine," Mayart said, confident she was talking to him, the old bastard.

I waved Makie's question away. "I'll be healed soon. I burnt through my reserves too quickly is all, so I'm paying for it now." I leaned on the seat back as I spoke.

My Psy Power was generated by a gland in my hypothalamus, but at that moment it was still slow, weak. The PP in the suit's weapon had suppressed my own PP-making abilities. What little I had left was almost all being used in the psychical process of healing. Consequently, I had almost nothing to use as a weapon.

I ignored the Shibuya scenery passing by the window and concentrated on PP recovery and powering back up.

V. McNorton, an American Black Guard, after taking four .38-caliber bullets directly in his heart, had healed himself in only four hours. I was not quite up to replicating that feat. Still, by the time we passed Aoyama University, gentle waves washed over my body from my hypothalamus. Another thirty minutes, and I would be fully healed.

Mayart's comment about becoming an essayist seemed to be the truth. He stared at the scenery through the window, scribbling away in a notebook with a ballpoint pen he had bought when we purchased Makie's clothes.

A quarter of the passengers left us in west Azabu, an

area packed with trendy cafés. The bus, which was primarily controlled by computer, whirred again into comfortable motion and set off into the night once more.

People who experience the city only during the daytime can't understand the changes that come over it when the sun sets. The moonlight gently washed the exhaustion from the buildings, and all the road signs and electricity poles seemed to take on a new life and new voice to communicate with the darkness. People walked along the sidewalks, not hunched and close because they are tired, but energetic because they hope to soon be home with their loved ones.

A voice came over the bus's intercom. "The next stop is Roppongi. We will make a twenty-minute stop. Please disembark, stretch your legs, and enjoy the sights."

The dull, scripted reading of this automated announcement elicited chuckles from a few of the passengers. Most of them prepared to disembark.

"What shall we do?" Makie asked, concerned.

I stood. "We'll get off." I wasn't fully recovered yet, but there was no helping that now.

Makie put a hand on my arm to stop me. "Rest. I'll look after Mayart."

"You're in just as bad shape as me—if not worse. We've taken every step we could to shake off the demons who know where we are, but there are plenty more out there. Taking a stroll through Roppongi is like asking them to step out and kill us."

"Let's not keep them waiting, then." Mayart already

had one foot on the steps that led from the bus. "I'll have more fun without you, anyway. If you are staying here, then I'm going."

I sighed. "That's that, then."

"That's that." Makie nodded, and all three of us headed outside. The bus had stopped in front of Seishido Books.

It was colder than I expected. The wind blew Makie's hair across my face, and the gentle scent of it stroked my nose.

Mayart didn't waste any time. "Any titty bars around here?"

I shook my head. "This isn't Kamata."

"Hah! What's a city without women? I love Kamata! I think I can find some fun here, too, though. Look at all the young señoritas!"

Mayart, mixing languages again, headed out in front of us toward the closest intersection.

"Hey, there's Macchi! And that's Sawaguchi with her! Oooh, it's a glamour photography session! I'll need autographs!"

His carefree attitude obviously came from living alone in the Italian mountains. He probably knew the models' names from magazines.

That he went boldly up to Sawaguchi, who stood with her manager, proved only that he was a man of brass balls. It was something of a surprise, though, to see her take the memo pad and ballpoint pen from Mayart, chatting happily with him the whole time, and sign her name. Even the cameraman didn't say anything. In fact, Macchi walked over as well, swinging her hips, and said, "Let me sign, too!"

When Mayart strolled back to Makie and me, obviously very pleased with himself, I was even more surprised when I saw what they had written. Not only an autograph, but their addresses and phone numbers were inscribed on the page in neat, beautiful script.

Mayart snatched the notebook from my hands. "Close your mouth, boy. My address book is crammed with information on the prettiest celebrities you can imagine—more than four hundred of them."

I felt like throwing up my hands. "Let's move on, then."

Mayart tucked the pad of paper under his arm, the pen in his pocket. "You'd better take me somewhere interesting!"

"How about a club? They'll have a bar there, too."

"It'd better be good!" Mayart wagged a finger at me.

I shrugged. "A disco?"

"Okay."

There was a place called With Me not far from where we were now, which I had visited two or three times with my office colleagues from the company. That would do for Mayart's purposes.

We started walking, and the presence of demons swirled all around us. There were at least ten of them nearby. However they all had official residential papers. A special procedure altered their presence, so I knew at a glance they were okay.

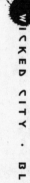

We started toward the Lower Building.

"I want an apple, too," Mayart piped up suddenly.

He really was a master of thinking up the most annoying little tasks. I knew the request wasn't arbitrary either. We were in front of a small twenty-four-hour supermarket.

It didn't look like I had a choice. I told Makie and Mayart to wait outside, and I went in. A member of the market's staff told me all the fruit was in the basement.

It reminded me of a supermarket I had once visited in Los Angeles. This place was smaller, but the atmosphere was exactly the same—including the fact it was almost empty.

I spotted a pile of red Fuji apples close to a freezer and went to collect one. Just as I reached my destination, a strange sound rang out behind me.

I turned, but there was no one there. Or they might have been there but hidden behind a mountain of canned food. I sensed a presence. It wasn't demonic, but it wasn't human either. I'd sensed this kind of presence before. But I couldn't recall when.

I waited a few seconds to see if the presence would reveal itself. "Come out."

There was no reply. I felt it, lingering behind a shelf of instant noodles. It intensified, and the wound in my stomach started to hurt.

Then I knew what it was—hatred.

I placed one of the apples into my pocket and nonchalantly grabbed my M29 from beneath my jacket. Something deep in my psyche was terribly afraid. It was like I knew, at least on some level, that I couldn't win bare-handed.

I cautiously headed toward the stairs. "I'm leaving, then."

As though signaled by my voice, a shelf of canned food collapsed. One of the cans shot past my head. I wasn't leaving just yet. No staff came rushing in, either, although the sound of the cans falling on the floor should have brought them running.

I approached the shelves. The presence moved, too—a black shadow passed across the gap between the shelves. I sped up and circled around the shelf where the shadow had gone. The shadow belonged to a woman, half-hiding behind the shelves.

The air was thick was her presence. The woman was only one shelf away from me now, watching. Watching me. I didn't have anything against her, of course, but she definitely had something against me, and that meant we were ultimately going to the same place. I closed off my own presence and softened my footsteps.

A number of cans fell toward me with a loud clatter. I took a step backwards in order to avoid them, and suddenly she was behind me. Even before I could be surprised by her unbelievable speed, my own feet moved. I kicked two cans, infused them with PP, and sent them flying behind me. One of them missed, but the second shot reported a dull thud. It didn't sound quite like metal impacting flesh, but still, success.

There was a rush of wind. I just caught the black shadow heading for the stairs. Her long green skirt flapped in the breeze. I jumped over a line of cans and gave chase.

I ran all the way to the stairs, but there was no sign of her. The lights from the ceiling coldly illuminated the space in which the two of us should have collided.

Where had she vanished to? I sensed no hint of an eldritch space that could have swallowed her.

I checked my surroundings, prepared for a surprise attack. At the bottom of the stairs there was a metal door; it probably led to either a storeroom or a cleaning cupboard.

There was a fifteen-centimeter gap between the door and the frame. Was that where she had gone? I thought carefully to the chase of a minute ago—I hadn't seen the door move. If the woman had gone through and pulled it shut, it would have made a noise when it banged against the frame. So . . . the woman had passed through a fifteen-centimeter gap to hide in there?

That was not enough to surprise me. This job quickly made even the most bizarre abilities and phenomena seem mundane. Once a demon had infiltrated Guard HQ disguised as water in the sewage pipes.

My hand still inside my jacket and wrapped around the M29, I moved toward the door. The gap was filled with darkness. I reached out with my left hand and touched it.

I was about to pull it open wider, when the clatter of footsteps descending the steps stopped me.

"What . . . what are you doing down here . . . sir? . . ."

It was the staff member from before. "What happened down here?"

"There was an earthquake." I raised my left hand, signaling for him to come no closer.

"What are you talking about?" The man threw up his arms, shouting. "Look at all these cans! How long do you think it took to line these up?! You'll be helping me restack . . ."

The man's voice trailed off. He must have seen the look in my eye.

I was firm but calm. "Go back upstairs."

"You . . . Who do you think you! . . ." The employee's resistance quickly petered out.

I made sure he had gone back upstairs before I pushed the door open. Inside was a small cupboard. The cleaning utensils and two cardboard boxes filled the small space, which was barely large enough for two adults to stand comfortably.

No one was there. The presence was gone, too.

The only other exit from the room was a hole in the back wall, approximately twenty centimeters in diameter. Perhaps it had been drilled as part of a plan to pass some sort of cables through?

It also apparently allowed the woman to escape. I put my eye to the hole, but the darkness within told me nothing.

I went back up the stairs, paid for the apple, then headed back onto the street. The member of the staff whom I had

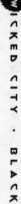

encountered below remained stony-faced and impassive the entire time.

Mayart badgered me the second I hit the sidewalk. "How long does it take to buy a single apple, eh? You're not fit to guard a fruit basket."

Hardly the greeting I would have desired right after a battle. Mayart apparently didn't recognize or care about what I had gone through to get his bit of fruit.

"Onward, to the club! Time to hit the dance floor!"

"But the bus will be leaving."

Mayart fixed me with a disgruntled expression. "You fool! We can get the next bus, so long as we hold on to our stubs. There's plenty of time until dawn. So come on!"

COILS OF VENGEANCE

PART SIX

1

THE INSIDE of With Me was packed to bursting with heat and music. The heat made the demonic presences even more evident, making it easier to locate them, but it also gave those skilled at concealing themselves an advantage.

Mayart danced crazily in the middle of the dim room, surrounded by young people. From his fevered dance steps you never would have guessed that he had almost been dead just a few hours ago. He was attracting his fair share of attention from those around him.

"He's a complex man, isn't he," Makie said seriously. She and I were seated as close to the dance floor as possible.

"You said it. I don't know if he's the real thing or not, but we're certainly in the presence of a powerful individual." I sipped my 7UP, then lit a cigarette, nodding. "I think I'm starting to like him. Look at him, after everything we've been through. I thought he was just a decoy at first, something to draw the demon's attention. But now I feel like protecting him no matter what. I'm going to get him to the signing tomorrow, even if he is a red herring."

Makie placed her hands on top of mine, and I knew at once that something was up. Her gaze looked almost mischievous, and her smile made her look like a teenage girl. I felt something distinctly human in her expression.

"You think it's okay to leave him in here?" she asked.

"Probably."

"Then shall we go outside?"

"What for?"

"Sex."

I looked closely at Makie. She did not turn away, but brazenly looked me right in the eye. "I want you inside me, right now."

"We're on duty." Although I was curt with her, I fully understood why she was suggesting it. My first reaction would have been to jump her right there, but my brain caught up with my cock before I could move. Ever since the suit in the basement of the factory had indicated my desire for her—to be honest, since I first met Makie in the Ueno station—I had been possessed by the desire to sleep with her, to share myself with her until we were practically indistinguishable, a single being. This was not the physical and intellectual joining of two people very much in love, though, but a purely physical, primal desire. For some reason, I felt sure we had to do it, that it was vital to do so.

Suddenly I remembered Mayart. I cast my senses out into the crowd to locate the old man. He was dancing, and he looked in my direction as he danced. Though his body moved with carefree exuberance, his expression was deadly serious, like no expression I had seen on his face. Then, I knew. . . . Mayart wanted us to do it, too.

Why would he want Makie and me to get it on, besides his lecherous tendencies toward sex at any opportunity? What would sex between me and Makie give birth to? The act itself, between one of the human world and one of the demonic, was not so rare a thing. However, in order for it to work at all, it was absolutely vital the demonic partner was able to completely cancel out his or her presence.

The act of sexual intercourse generally carried with it a particularly high emotional state. If the human partner was a normal human being, both their body and mind would be exposed to the overbearing power of the other side. Many of the humans who coupled with those from the other side either fell ill or simply faded away afterwards.

The highest ranking humans had negotiated with their counterparts on the other side, requesting that intercourse between humans and demons be prohibited unless the demon partner had both the capacity for self-control and had powers that were not harmful to the human psyche.

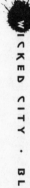

Despite the laws put in place to prevent it, the chain of poor fools who walked the path of destruction, unable to resist the lure of sex with those from the other side, remained long and unbroken.

Many of the Black Guard had experienced otherworld intercourse, with a number of them also succumbing to symptoms, but for the most part it proved little more than a wild diversion. I had taken a succubus up on her offer of a little fun while in a public bath in Paris, and the experience had pushed my mind so far, I almost committed suicide. When such trysts carried dangers even for those like me, who had Psychic Powers and could control them, the risks to normal people amounted to ripping out the roots of their humanity.

I understood all this and yet I remained unsure. I was a Black Guard, which meant I knew better than anyone the risks of sharing myself with Makie. So why did I still desire her so strongly? And why was Mayart seemingly so keen on this outcome, too?

"Come on," Makie said, her voice thick. "Let's go. I want you to do me . . . now."

That alone was enough to turn me on, yet I gently removed my hands from hers.

"Coward."

"That's reality for you." Bitterness swelled inside me. In Shibuya, I had felt secure in the knowledge that Mayart was in the Hospital. But now that safety was gone. We couldn't afford to take our eyes off him.

She pushed her lower lip out in a half pout. It was prob-

HIDEYUKI KIKUCHI

ably intended to be cute, but did nothing for her. "You don't like me? . . ."

The question was surprisingly direct, and I fought the wry smile that threatened to cross my lips. Makie had probably never asked that question before, and was unlikely ever to ask it again.

"That isn't it. We are on duty."

"Well." Makie withdrew her hands from the table and looked over at Mayart.

"Hey, baby, how you doin'?" A cocky, cheerful voice called out from behind us. I looked over my shoulder. Three young men, seventeen or eighteen, stood behind us, all wearing flashy shirts and loose slacks.

They weren't demons . . . but still, I couldn't be sure. There were so many from the high levels out tonight, I couldn't always trust my senses. I had learned that the hard way.

One of them stepped forward. "Had a fight with your boyfriend, have you? We'll entertain you, if you like."

Makie ignored them. The brush-off must have made them mad. The stupidest-looking among them reached out and grabbed her shoulder. He gave me a meaningful look and said, "Look, he doesn't mind. We'll teach you a few new tricks that you can show him later."

"You will?" Makie said sweetly. She gently touched the youth's hand, and he stiffened.

He grinned like a Cheshire cat. "You'll have a good time, I can promise you that."

Makie, smiling back at him, wrapped her slender fingers

WICKED CITY · BLACK GUARD

around the moron's fat- and sugar-fed digits and started to apply pressure. The sound of bones breaking was clear, even above the music.

Her victim tried to pull away, but Makie did not let go. When she finally did release him, he crumpled to the floor. The faces of his two friends quickly turned nasty.

"You bitch," they said in unison.

I stopped Makie from getting up and instead stood up myself. One of them was thin, 170 centimeters tall, but the other had a neck thicker than my own. He was *wide*, and the way he stood indicated he could handle himself in a fight.

He cracked his knuckles threateningly. "Sit back down, or we'll be taking this outside."

"I doubt you'll thank me for this, but know that you're getting off lightly." Before either of them could do anything, I jabbed my little finger into the big man's sternum.

It sank into his body up to the knuckle. I treated him to enough PP to knock him out for the rest of the night. Then I kicked my left leg behind me, ending the thin man's attempt to jump me with his quiet collapse to the floor. I dropped the big guy on top of him and turned to the first victim, still clutching his hand, and ordered him to drag his friends away before returning to my seat.

"That was kind of you."

Makie did not look at me as she replied. For this woman, what had just happened was little more than an insect chasing off other, lesser insects. If I had not stepped in, she would either have ripped the three idiots limb from limb or destroyed their minds.

I lifted my glass of 7UP, ice now melted, and took a swallow. Finally the only cheerful member of our party returned to the table.

"Glad to see you two looking so happy!" Mayart's sarcasm wasn't quite so heavy as usual. "Here, let me introduce you—this is my new friend, Meg."

I was confronted with a round, smiling face pressed between slender fingers.

"I'm Megumi! Nice to meet ya!"

Makie's blank expression when she met Megumi was priceless.

Mayart clapped his hands. "This has made my night, it really has! She's going to join us on the tour."

"Hold on a moment." Even I knew my voice was overly harsh. "We haven't got a handle on this situation yet. A large percentage of the Tokyo population is gunning for your neck tonight."

Mayart seemed taken aback, but persisted. "Oh, come on . . . we've gotten this far. One more isn't going to make any difference."

"We don't have the resources to watch out for the girl, too," I argued. "You by yourself are proving to be quite enough."

"Oh, there's no need to worry about me," Megumi chirped. She wore a tiny top—little more than a bra—that barely covered a fine pair of rounded tits. With one hand,

she swept back her short hair, pearls of sweat glinting along her neck. She was an experienced club girl. "I'll just tag along. I won't get in the way!"

Mayart beamed at her. "See? She'll be fine!"

"It is almost half past one." I managed to keep my anger under control and not voice the misgivings I had over the whole idea of Megumi "tagging along." "Just over three hours until dawn. Are you sure you wouldn't rather spend it with just me and Makie?"

Megumi was persistent. "Oh, come on! You won't even know I'm here!" Her eyes sparkled, and her thighs, wrapped tightly in criminally short hot pants, rubbed together. "Where else could I go but wherever this wonderful old man goes? And you, too. He's such a sweetie, it's only natural I want to follow him! Isn't that right, darling?"

"That's right! Only natural!" Mayart gave a lecherous laugh, his bony old hands sliding along the girl's thighs. The laugh certainly wasn't an act—this man was really a horny old bastard. Once again. I wondered if that meant he couldn't also be the real Mayart. I had never heard he was a monk or anything, after all.

Mayart kept rubbing Megumi's thighs as he spoke to me in the demanding tone I had come to associate with him. "We're continuing the bus tour, anyway. I've promised to spend some time in a hotel with this girl, too. Come on, then—let's move."

Mayart pointed toward the doorway, and the girl—Megumi—vanished into the jumble of dancing people.

Makie turned to me as we followed the cheerfully bouncing Mayart toward the exit. "That's one smooth old man. Let's keep him on the bus for as long as we can. We'll have to be careful to make sure he doesn't use his sleeping trick on us."

I remained silent, unsure of what I might say if I opened my mouth.

It was almost two in the morning, but the street was still jam-packed with people. What were all these people doing at this hour, and when did they plan on going home?

We crossed an intersection and waited at the bus stop. It didn't take long for the bus to show up. People piled from the doors at the rear. We climbed aboard and found one passenger still on board. It was a woman wearing sunglasses and a suit. She sat at the back of the bus and looked forward, instead of out of the window.

Her presence was not demonic. She was human. But I still couldn't be sure. There were at least two demons somewhere that could totally conceal their presence, making themselves appear human. Just in case, Makie and I flanked Mayart, Makie in front, me behind.

Just as the bus was about to pull out, a voice called from outside, and the girl from the club climbed aboard. She had purchased a ticket that allowed her to travel on every route.

She seemed, well . . . okay, she was dumb. Her clothing was unchanged from back in the disco, more flesh than material, and a cloth bag hung from her hand.

"You almost missed me!" she said with a hint of nastiness. She dropped down next to Mayart. "Oh, is this seat taken?"

Although it may have been better just to get rid of her, the bus was in motion again, and upsetting Mayart was likely to make him run off once more. I didn't trust him to stay put. After all, this was a man who used an enemy attack as cover to escape and find a piece of ass. And for all that he appeared to be an obvious decoy, there was something about him that defied all logic.

The bus continued into the night. The streets outside were less crowded now; the throngs of people looking for food had been replaced with tired clubbers heading toward after-hours cafés or bars. When the subway lines started up at 5 A.M., the trains would finally carry them all home. I once heard someone joke that the early morning sunlight simply sucked the little vigor that remained from their bodies.

I was finally starting to feel the gap between myself and younger people. I was hardly over the hill, but still, with more than five years between me and those who surrounded me, I couldn't avoid noticing the obvious differences between us.

The world was changing. What would the next generation of Black Guard bring?

Tension suddenly ran through the interior of the bus. It came from me and Makie. In the same instant, everything outside the bus's windows was swallowed in darkness.

"W-what's happening?" Mayart's eyes widened.

"Don't stop!" I shouted at the driver. The sudden change seemed to disturb him, but the man lifted his foot from the brake pedal. I placed the barrel of my M29 against his neck.

His knuckles turned white on the steering wheel. "W-what're you doing?!"

"Keep going, full speed, through this darkness! Don't stop!"

"Y-you're insane! I can't see a thing out there!"

"We can still escape before the space solidifies, if we hurry! If we get stuck in here again, it's going to be a pain to get out!"

Makie's voice was like a knife through the tension in the air. "They're coming."

I looked up. White spheres appeared ahead of us, in the depths of the darkness where the streets of Roppongi should have been.

"Smash through them!" I shouted, pressing my gun farther into the flesh of the driver's neck.

The driver had no choice but to press the accelerator as hard as he could. The spheres bounced, one after another, against the windshield. The last one stuck to the glass. Then the window started to melt, and I recognized the creature. The demon from Kamata!

It couldn't have picked us up in the Roppongi disco. It must have been following us since Shibuya. I started infusing my body with PP, placed my hand on the melting glass, and sent the attached demon flying off into the night.

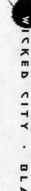

WICKED CITY · BLACK GUARD

I glanced down—there were spheres on the road below us. If they melted the tires or engine, we would be finished. Although it was probably a waste of ammo, I poked my .44 Magnum out the window and fired into the darkness, toward where the spheres seemed to be originating. The demon shouldn't be aware of my M29, or the PP bullets it was loaded with.

I didn't know the range. Did not know the location, either. One of the spheres was now attached to the bottom of the bus.

I pulled the trigger, and a pillar of fire sliced through the darkness. Two, three more times.

It looked like I was getting results. I heard a squeal and then a scream from the darkness.

The spheres stopped coming. I fired a final shot into the sphere stuck to the bus, splattering it into oblivion. I told the driver to just keep going. The engine roared, seemingly still intact. But the darkness continued.

"I don't think we made it in time," Makie said from behind me. "The eldritch space has solidified. Leave this to me."

"You don't have that tool with you, do you?"

"There's another way."

"There is?"

"Don't worry. I'll be okay. But we'll need to take some steps first."

Anxiety grew in my chest about letting Makie do anything, after what had happened to her in the factory. But there did not appear to be any other way to escape the space.

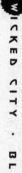

"Everyone, gather in once place. Quickly," Makie said.

I returned to my seat and looked behind me at Mayart. He was there, but someone else was missing.

"Where's Megumi?" I asked Mayart roughly. His face was stretched with tension.

"Huh? She was just here . . . then she got up and went . . . to the back of the bus. . . ."

I looked around. There was only the woman wearing the sunglasses. But she was different, somehow. Her stomach was swollen.

My blood froze in my veins. No . . . Could this woman be the same one I had noticed getting on our first bus in Shibuya?

Sunglasses . . . What better way to hide one eye than to hide them both? I hurried to the woman's side and pointed my M29 at her. There was no response.

Makie shouted, "What are you doing? The more time we waste, the more difficult this is going to be! If we wait much longer, I won't be able to get us out of here unaided!"

"Hold on." I swung my M29 down, hitting the woman's shoulder.

There was no resistance. Her suit crumpled inward easily. No, more than her suit—her face also withered and crumbled away.

I removed the sunglasses and was greeted by two empty sockets. The right was human sized, but the left was uneven, with rough edges, as though something had torn it out. Or a .44 Magnum had been shot into it.

The snake! A string of events all clicked into place,

starting with Azabu. I had destroyed the snake's eye, and in anger it had come after us, swearing revenge. It had turned into a woman wearing a green skirt in Shibuya, and attacked me in the supermarket in Roppongi, where it had fled through the hole in the wall—which had been the perfect size and shape for snake.

Then it had turned into the woman before us and absorbed Megumi. . . . This was nothing but a cast-off skin. So where was—

Two screams sounded behind me. One was Mayart, the other the driver.

I turned to an almost unbelievable sight.

2

MAKIE, THE cold demon Makie, was frozen in place, fear covering her face. A thick snake with mottled blue-green skin was wrapped around her torso, gradually tightening.

I instinctively pointed my M29 at the creature. The snake's head moved up and around to use Makie's head as a shield, fixing me with red eyes that blazed with loathing.

"Try anything and I'll swallow her, headfirst," the snake said. "Look, she's about to lose her mind, just having me wrapped around her."

The snake licked Makie's face with a flickering red

tongue. Makie threw her head back. Instead of fear or repulsion, I couldn't help but think she looked more like she was in ecstasy. The snake's tongue passed over Makie's eyelids and face and then across her lips.

Reason returned to Makie's expression, and she started to desperately turn her head away. The snake squeezed tighter, holding Makie's face in place. Makie tightly closed her mouth—we had both worked out what the snake wanted.

The snake seemed happy to take its time. It looked at me with blazing eyes and laughed. The tongue moved slowly, lingeringly along the quivering white throat.

Makie let out a gasp—a sensual sound. After the first one escaped, there was no stopping them. The sounds of her resistance to the ministrations of the snake continued to seep through her sealed lips. This was not the only attack launched by the snake. Its body continued to coil tighter. Rubbing her breasts with his constricted body did not seem enough for the snake, and his tail lifted upward and slid between her legs.

A beautiful woman being ravaged by a snake—such a sinful, despicable sight; how many times had the ages been subjected to it?

Unable to resist the snake's attacks on her throat and body, Makie finally opened her mouth. The fine tongue probed her gums and passed into her mouth. Makie let out something like a scream as it started to twine with her own tongue.

The sound of their sticky kissing filled the bus. The

snake's tongue worked its magic. It wound around, stroked, and rubbed her tongue. Whatever it was doing to Makie brought tears to her eyes.

The snake was so preoccupied with bringing Makie to the brink of insanity that it did not notice her right hand breaking free. As her hand slipped from between the evil coils, I dashed to Mayart's side.

Makie's white fingers straightened, and before the snake even had time to realize something was happening, Makie had plunged her hand deep into her own chest, just above her right breast.

Blue blood sprayed out. As soon as it touched the snake's skin, the creature started to give off smoke the same color as the blood. Then it started to melt. His tongue unwrapped itself from Makie's.

"Stay back!" Her shout stopped me in my tracks. "Stay with Mayart! Don't move! I'm going to break out of this space!"

"Wait!" I couldn't stand by and watch her bleed all over, and then expend more energy breaking us out of the eldritch space. "Let me help."

She shook her head. "I told you! It will be okay. I'll keep both of you safe!"

Makie turned, more blue blood flying from the wound in her chest. This time the blood pierced through one of the bus windows and spread into the night.

The darkness—the very darkness itself—turned blue.

The color of this new world started to bleed into everything, washing over Makie, the snake, me, and Mayart. A

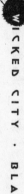

WICKED CITY · BLACK GUARD

terrible chill cut through me. Now fully aware of the side effects to using irregular means for breaking free of an eldritch space, I tumbled into my own darkness.

Someone slapped my cheek. It was an unrestrained blow, which gave me some idea who it might be.

We had yet to meet, but I knew I was right. A woman stood amid the darkness of my dim vision. She was as beautiful as Makie, but the blatant cruelty displayed on her face marred the visage.

This had to be the final of the big three. I tried to move my arms and legs, and soon realized how pointless that was.

I was totally powerless.

"Give it up. You've been injected with a drug that paralyzes your abilities."

The woman's voice was stunningly beautiful. Her laugh continued to ring in the air long after it had ended, the beauty gradually falling from it until only cruelty remained.

"Taki of the Black Guard. I finally have you. Do not expect your death to be a pleasant one."

I was busy checking my surroundings. We appeared to be on the corner of some empty land somewhere. The first breeze of autumn brushed my cheek. Buildings in the distance sparkled with lights. There were still stars in the sky, meaning it wasn't dawn just yet. It must not be long after our escape from the eldritch space. Hopefully we were still near Roppongi, but the shock of escaping the space could have bounced us anywhere. That must have been what Makie was worried about.

"Where's Makie?" I asked.

"She vanished during your little escape. Who knows where she's been kicked to? I have my underlings searching for her and that annoying Mayart."

"She got away? What a shame."

"I'd worry about yourself if I was you," the woman said in a high-pitched voice. Her body shook, probably in anticipation of tearing me limb from limb.

It wasn't worth trying to resist. I looked at the sky.

"You may not know it, but something terrible is proceeding in the shadows of this world," the woman went on. She brushed the shoulder of her funeral suit. "I want to ask you something, which is why you're not dead yet. Have you had sexual relations with that traitor . . . with Makie yet?"

Even under these circumstances, I couldn't help but smile wryly. "Why is everyone so interested in my love life all of a sudden? But yeah, I did her."

Despair, plain and simple, spread across the woman's face. "We are too late. . . . If only I had acted sooner. . . . We should have killed you two first, rather than aiming for Mayart."

"What are you talking about? Your friend in Shibuya said something similar. If you're going to kill me anyway, how about filling me in first?"

I was trying to buy some time, but also checking the

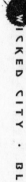

surrounding darkness. I moved my eyes, nothing more. There were plenty of demons out there. I was in a grassy area so wide, I was unable to place where it might be in Tokyo. The long grass gently waved in the wind around us. Among the stems were countless twisted, demonic forms. A full-force Militant gathering.

Why were they more interested in whether Makie and I had sex than they were in Mayart? Makie and I did appear to be connected in some primal, sexual way, but I didn't know anything more than that.

"We shall proceed with the surgery," the woman proclaimed quietly, ominously. She looked at me with unbridled disdain. "I need to ask your body something. We have all the doctors and nurses we could ever need. Look."

Eldritch wind swept across the grass, marking the appearance of more demons. None of them were cloaked in human form. In the last three hundred years, the instances of demons appearing in their natural demonic state could be counted on one hand. The most recent recorded sighting was on December 4, 1906, in Yamagata prefecture. The truth of that incident was a hot topic for debate between Historical Investigations and the Data Cell, and was unlikely to be resolved any time soon.

It looked like I was about to undergo a highly rare and possibly valuable experience. The works *Ten Thousand Teachings of Buddha* and *Clear Water of Knowledge on the Wild Plain*, penned by the two great saints Gautama Buddha and Jesus Christ respectively, had already precisely detailed the natural physical appearance of demons. Of course, these books weren't exactly on the shelves in the library.

The creatures that surrounded me now, so foul as to corrupt the very air itself, were bizarre and twisted enough to instill fear even into me, one who had witnessed hundreds of their human-shaped incursions into our world. The things we—meaning humans—called tentacles or feelers had been given such names only in order to cram them into our limited perceptions. Their feelers may in fact have been energy changers: their horns may actually have been thought centers.

For now, however, I had more important things to worry about than redefining how we described them. All those around me as I lay prone on the ground were of shapes and colors that could not be described by human language.

One of those closest to me, a mantislike creature, was covered in blades, needles poking from its joints. It sprayed liquid onto the grass, causing it to give off a disgusting rotten smell. Yet the grass grew greener.

The number of slimy tentacles that reached toward my body rivaled the number of blades of grass around me. If a normal person was touched by so many demons at once, they would surely be driven to insanity and madness. Each and every one was a different shape, color, and size. It was an overload of bizarre information that would crush the mind of a regular person. The demon's bodies

ignored all physical rules, lacked any uniform structure. The very existence of the demons themselves, with their own realm, was almost impossible to reconcile to the average human.

Bizarre shapes, without mouths, without eyes, looked me over, and sounds that were not speech filled the darkness.

The woman raised her right hand. A number of the shadows broke off from the pack and gathered at my right side. They undulated and writhed for several moments. It looked like they were melting together, like scoops of ice cream left in the sun. The transformation was swift, and when they were finished, the coral-like, thorny horns of the fused-together demons plunged into my body.

A glowing soft-bodied organ slid from inside the combined demon and onto the ground, which looked odd to me—like the earth was melting. No, the ground had not melted; the demon was fusing with that, too. The organ started to glow, and then dozens of stalks, bizarrely shaped, thrust from within, breaking through its skin. In the same instant, the coral thorns that pierced my body moved, and I screamed in pain.

The woman gave a high-pitched laugh as my vision clouded. "How does that feel? This is demonic surgery! Does it hurt? Oh, does it burn? We cannot lessen your pain, you understand. If we did, your cells would no longer give us the information we require from them. Do try to put up with the pain, and don't worry. Even if you're reduced to just your filthy brain, I'll be sure to leave you alive."

"What are you hoping to achieve by ripping me apart? It isn't going to make me want to sleep with you." I tried my best to sound nonchalant, but my voice was little more than a whisper. I wasn't sure the woman had heard me.

I turned back to the melded pile of demon, my primary torturer. The remainder of the coral thorns jabbed into the runny earth beneath it, and the central life-form started to glow again. Tubes, like the kind used to hold the brightly colored neon gas for signs at strip joints back in Kamata, reached out from the writhing mass, toward the woman.

Through the haze of my fading consciousness and desperately clinging to some tiny bit of my Psy Power, it occurred to me that this was some kind of demonic-style diagnostic device.

The woman watched the glowing tubes for a while; then her brow furrowed. "Hmm, nothing in particular. . . . Aside from exceptionally high PP, he's no different from any other Black Guard. So why did they choose *him and Makie*?"

Surprise at her last statement, along with another stab of pain, slapped some reason back into me. *Choose?* . . . What was she talking about? Was the reason behind Makie's and my selection to guard Mayart really enough for them to go to these lengths?

The woman rubbed the tips of her fingers together, pensive. "We'll have to take the examination to the genetic level. There must be something we've missed. Begin to dismember him."

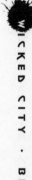

WICKED CITY · BLACK GUARD

The thorns, still biting deep inside me, started to move again. It was not the fire of my flesh tearing but the overflowing pain that made me bite down on my lip. The taste of blood flooded my mouth. My muscles and organs were shredding, being ripped asunder, and I felt myself slipping into the dark of unconsciousness. . . .

The pain suddenly stopped. The hooks in my flesh released. I felt a wave of energy, without heat or sound . . . PP!

The wind picked up, and suddenly the body of the demonic surgeon shattered into a thousand pieces. There had been no sign of what caused the explosion—not a gunshot or a hail of stones; it had to have been a long-range blast of pure Psy Power. There were less than five people in Japan who could have done it.

The breeze turned into a wall of flame, clearing away the surrounding demons and filling the air with voiceless screams.

My face was hot. With the thorns gone, the PP flowed from my hypothalamus and began to revive my cells. Someone was lending me strength.

The second I could, I stood, smashing off the remaining barbs. Attackers came from my left and right. I smashed through a furry, fanged face in front of me and leaped into the air.

I cleared three meters, but quickly fell to the grass. I had yet to recover enough PP to fight them head-on. I ran, keeping my body low.

Something flew over my head, ringing in the air, the wind of it blowing strands of my hair as it passed.

I smoothly pulled up two clumps of grass from the roots using my left hand, and a pebble with my right. I rolled the pebble on my palm and infused it with PP. My effective range when launching an attack using nothing but Psy Power was limited to three meters. Training made little difference—even the strongest PP user could either project it, or could not. A Black Guard in Havana called Gilbert, for example, was a long-range specialist, able to kill a target instantly at over twenty meters.

I hardly had what I would call sufficient PP, but the stone was now fairly powerful. I waited . . . just another half a second. . . . I threw the pebble and one of the clumps of grass into the air above me. A chill ran down my spine, and I felt rather than heard the stone impact the target. Quick reflexes were one of the benefits of Psychic Power. Though I currently lacked a great quantity of it, I was still able to react almost pre-cognitively. When I was at full power, my reactions were at least three times faster than those of a normal human being.

Shredded grass drifted down around my ears, cleanly cut in two as it floated back to earth. Something very sharp would be required to cause such clean cuts, and not necessarily a knife. The pebble returned to the earth with a dull thud, and I slowly, carefully wrapped my hand around it. The demon behind me shifted, ready to launch another attack.

Eldritch power shifted violently behind me, as if someone had shoved the demon away. Whoever it was who had saved me, they were fighting with the demons now. I was curious to see who it was, but allowing myself to be distracted would swiftly get me killed. I had no idea where my enemy was. I couldn't sense her presence. Yes, it had to be her, the last of the big three.

I leaped out of the grass and spread my senses in all directions. The evil intent that accompanied the attack, the demon's hatred blasting my senses, saved my life. I could almost see the arch drawn by invisible power as it headed toward me. Not with my eyes, but with my instincts. Avoiding it while hanging in midair was impossible. It tore into my chest and smashed me to the ground. Earth, grass, and leaves showered down on top of me.

Something stood about five meters beyond my right foot. It was, as expected, the same demonic woman. She pushed herself through the grass toward me, dragging her left leg, which had been damaged by my Psy missile when she had attacked me earlier.

The black pupils of her eyes had changed to blood-red, and a crescent moon mouth lined with terrible teeth had opened beneath her throat. Her breathing was ragged. Apparently she was forced to obey some of our natural laws.

"I was only a step away from victory, before I was so rudely interrupted. But you'll be finished here. But before that, allow me to compliment you on your attack."

"I'm glad you liked it," I offered with a wink.

The woman bared her teeth in a snarl. Her presence sliced toward me, sharp as steel. I caught it on the other clump of grass, still in my hand. I threw the pebble again. It smashed into the woman's throat, passing clear out the other side. There was the sound of bones breaking, and the woman's head slumped backwards.

A fountain of yellow liquid erupted from the entrance wound. It rained down on the grass, and the vegetation started to wither and then melt and die.

The woman swung her undamaged leg at my chest. I blocked the attack with my left arm, and a strange shock ran down it. The Psy Power in her leg passed through my arms and directly impacted my sternum.

I doubled over at the sudden onslaught of dizziness and cold, vomiting. But even as I vomited, I leaped forward and stuck out my right hand.

My hand found the sticky, fluid-spilling hole, and I reached inside. The woman couldn't move—I had hold of her windpipe. I held her body down with my left hand and sank my right down inside her to a place just above her breasts, beneath her mouth.

I shoved my fingers diagonally upward. The internal vein of corrosive fluid ruptured, spilling the content within. The mouth in the woman's throat opened, and I saw my fingers inside. The same yellow fluid swelled from the wound, filling her oral cavity. White smoke began to cover the woman's throat and head, eating her flesh.

I made sure she was finished before hopping back. Long yellow threads clung to my fingers—they were hot.

The strength suddenly left my knees. Dizziness struck me, welling up from my lungs. The smoke from the corrosive fluid was suddenly all around me. Why hadn't I realized it was poisonous?

I held my breath and started to run.

"You can't escape. That smoke will chase you to your grave."

In the corner of my eye I thought I saw the melting lips of the dying demon form a final cold smile.

3

THE WOMAN hadn't been lying. After running for a few meters, I looked behind me to see the white smoke following as though caught up in my wake. It moved against the natural wind, like a ghost, closing in for the kill. It shook with anger, rage, and sadness—the spite of a woman.

I checked my surroundings. There was no indication of demonic presence, or of the one who had saved me. It felt as though they were still nearby, but I shook my head. I should be running instead of hanging around here to search for whoever it was. I couldn't very well risk an inhabited area, so I turned my back on the lights of the city and ran.

I quickly reached a fairly wide path, running alongside a

large lot of vacant land. I looked around for some indication of where I was and spotted a large sign about a meter ahead.

The empty land belonged to the city. It looked as though a basic power grid had been laid down. The sign said I was in Arakawa ward, in East Ogu. At least I was still within city limits. My next problem—how could I escape my smoky pursuer?

It had already crossed the fringe of the path, sliding inexorably toward me. A nonliving entity possessed of both the intent and hatred of a scorned woman. Why were there so many demons like this?

I crossed the road and headed into the empty plot on the other side. I quickly discovered there was unlikely to be any escape. The sign that had informed me of my location started to bubble, thick wooden supports and all. It melted into putrid liquid and crumbled away. The smoke was getting closer.

I ran, and soon heard water. Knowing approximately where I was, I identified it as the Sumida River. I wondered if I could escape the smoke by swimming across the river, or if I even had the strength to traverse it.

Another twenty meters of running brought the banks into view. The river was right in front of me. Its surface sparkled like silver scales in the moonlight.

I dashed down to the edge. On a small wharf about five meters to my right, I spotted a very welcome sight. A boat. ARAKAWA WATER AUTHORITY was painted on the side in wide letters.

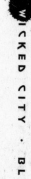

I clambered aboard, passed the oars through their metal hoops, and then cast off the mooring line. As I pushed away from the bank, I looked up toward the top.

The smoke appeared, caressing the grass as it came.

The river was just over seven meters wide. I started to row with all my might. Using PP, my speed was considerable, faster even than a professional rower. In less than two seconds, I was in the center of the river—and that was against the flow of the current.

I controlled the oars to prevent being swept away and prepared to see the smoke meet the water.

The smoke stopped by the waterside, hesitating. As though it was unsure.

But only for a moment. The cloud moved forward, and suddenly it appeared to expand. This increase in volume was not part of my pursuer, but gouts of steam.

The water started to boil. Or rather to *melt,* the same way that the sign had. As the eldritch smoke made its way across the water, the clouds of steam rose higher and higher everywhere it touched, eventually covering the moon itself.

It was going to contaminate the entire river. This could lead to years of extensive pollution. I had to get it out of the river.

I relaxed the oars and let the current carry me ten or so meters, then used the oars to cross to the bank. The smoke changed direction again, following me.

Panic gripped me, and I started to run along the riverbank, but my legs were heavy. Dawn had to be close. . . .

Just as my panic started to be replaced by despair, I heard the engine of a car beyond the riverbank. Could it be help?

But my hope was quickly crushed. The presence that poured over the banks was clearly demonic.

WICKED CITY · BLACK GUARD

THE SIGNING CEREMONY

PART SEVEN

I

I TURNED around. The smoke was less than three meters away. A final, desperate choice flashed into my brain. Subdue the other demons and force them to tell me how to get rid of the eldritch smoke. Of course, I would be unable to surprise them.

A presence crested the bank. There was no time to act; I was sure I was finished.

But the shadow that appeared on the riverbank was decidedly human. "There!" the shadow shouted. "It's Velma eldritch smoke. Taki, are you here?"

It was not the call of an enemy.

Another voice tried to find its way through my confusion.

"We're Tranquillites. The Supervisory Section sent us with orders to rescue you. You can come out, it is safe! Your pursuer will be finished here!"

It was still a gamble—they could still be demons and the whole thing a trap. But there was no other choice. I climbed up the bank.

Two men stood there, both wearing suits and porkpie hats. One of them waved me over. "This way. Into the car."

I headed down the other side of the bank. A third man stood in front of the car, operating a device that I had seen before.

"How's it going? Dawn is almost upon us," one of the men asked their companion.

"All green," he replied. He did not take his eyes from the device. "The generator is at 99.9 percent capacity. Quick, get in the car."

One of the men opened the door, and I was bundled into the backseat. The others climbed in and closed the doors. The window glass was tinted so that no one could see in from outside.

I shifted uncomfortably in my seat. "I'm not keen on running away. Isn't there any way to stop that smoke?"

The oldest-looking man, sitting in the front passenger seat, turned around and looked at me. "Leave it to us. We can't destroy it, but we can seal it away. A -ha! An eldritch space!"

"Here it comes," the man sitting next to me said in a low voice. The exterior of the car was surrounded in the white mist.

"Don't worry," the older man said. "This car has a specially treated exterior. We can last ten minutes, easy, before we start to melt."

"I'm activating it . . . ," the man in the passenger seat said, ". . . now!"

The change did not occur outside the vehicle, as I expected, but in the exterior appearance of the men. For a moment they were covered in scientifically impossible, entirely demonic protrusions, and in the next they had returned to normal. Their true forms had been laid bare in the presence of dimensional changes. They weren't inside human bodies, at least, and so I felt I could at least believe them. I couldn't trust them yet, however.

"All clear," the man in the passenger seat said. "A fifty-meter radius. Break out at high speed, and I'll close it."

"Then the Processing Section can do their thing," the man beside me replied.

The driver finally spoke: "Here we go. This is going to be fast. You might want to hold on to something back there."

A few seconds later, we were speeding along Aoyama, heading for Shibuya.

We smashed out of the eldritch space, leaving the Velma smoke in our dust. Our sudden appearance in the middle of Aoyama caused two nearby cars to crash into each other, but that was the only ill effect of our trip.

I smoothed my clothing. "How did you know where I

was? Don't tell me the Supervisory Section keeps tabs on me, too?"

"To tell you the truth, the Supervisory Section was unaware of the danger that you, personally, were in," the oldest of the men replied. "We received a tip about that location and the presence of the smoke from the Diplomatic Section."

"By who, specifically?"

The man shrugged. "I was not told. Judging by the reaction to the information by our superiors, it was someone big. Definitely in the same league as Mr. Mayart."

I looked out of the window for a moment at the buildings and their lights sliding by. "So . . . where are you taking me now?"

"You'll see when we get there."

Without any further conversation, we eventually arrived at a small apartment building behind Aoyama University.

"This is the office of the Crossovers Section," the older man said. He handed me a key. "You'll have to see for yourself what awaits you inside. It may be Mr. Mayart, and it may not."

"What about you?"

"Our work has just begun. Militants and power-crazy humans are causing no end of trouble right now. We can't afford to stay and protect you. Take care."

"Thanks for everything."

I offered him my hand. The man looked at me and the extended limb in surprise for a moment, then stiffly shook it. I thanked the other two men and climbed out onto the sidewalk. The door closed and the car melted away into the darkness.

I went into the apartment building's lobby and got into the elevator. The number on the key tag was 44. A very demonic number.

The building was small but expensive—high rent. I took the elevator to the fourth floor and walked along a long white corridor until I arrived at the appropriate door. Without pressing the buzzer I inserted the key and turned it.

An elegant woman, dressed all in black, stood in the middle of a living room filled with expensive-looking furniture. She must have sensed my presence because she turned. Black eyes danced with a mysterious light, and she started to laugh.

"You're safe," Makie said quietly. Her voice was cold as usual, unbending.

"Yeah, though I still don't know exactly how. What happened to you after we ditched the snake?"

"Supervisory Section picked me up at an intersection in Tameike. That's what the men from there told me, anyway. I don't remember much."

I crossed my arms over my chest. "Someone told them where we were. Where's Mayart?"

Makie shook her head. "Still missing. The Supervisory Section is continuing the search for him."

"Someone saved me from a bunch of demons, someone I couldn't see. Maybe it was the same someone who

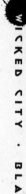

told the Supervisory Section where to find us. Could it have been Mayart?"

Makie said nothing. I slumped onto the leather sofa and reached into my jacket pocket, but pulled my hand out again. Forget cigarettes—there wasn't even a handkerchief in there. That woman had taken everything.

"There are cigarettes on the table."

I opened a silver cigarette case and whistled. They were my brand. "No expense spared, huh. Is all this your doing?" I lit up with what looked like a solid-gold lighter and took a deep breath. It felt like ages since I had last enjoyed the familiar smoke in my lungs.

"Hardly a setting fit for such cheap smokes." Makie perched on the edge of the table.

I averted my gaze from her slender figure—her dress clung to all her delicious curves. It was making me crazy. "We'll get out of here once I'm done."

"Why?"

"Our mission isn't finished yet. If we just sit back, smoke, and leave everything to the Supervisory Section, we'll have to write our resignations, too."

"Maybe we have a different mission."

"What?"

Makie stood without a sound. A sweet scent wafted toward me. "Look at me . . . Taki . . ."

She sounded almost sad. I turned my head toward her just as she placed her hand on the shoulder of her gown. Like a rippling black wave, the garment fell to the floor, leaving Makie totally naked. Her body was a combination of pure, unsullied virgin and sultry, voluptuous vixen. The sight of her stimulated me beyond all reason, and the inside of my head turned white. A scent that wasn't bodily musk or perfume but something else, more primal, filled the air. Even as I breathed it in, hot thighs climbed atop me. Sweet, soft lips pressed down on my own, her moist tongue probing boldly into my mouth.

2

WE FINALLY drew apart, and Makie looked at me with eyes full of lust. Perhaps it was the shade of sadness that I saw behind it that stayed my hand, even amid the blazing, relentless flames of desire.

"Take me, Taki . . . now, take me."

When I did not respond, she gently took my hand and placed it between her thighs. Her pussy was already hot and wet, and the sensation of my fingers slipping inside her ran directly to my own crotch. I was hard almost instantly.

"You still don't understand? I'm not doing this simply out of lust. Sex between us carries a much more important meaning."

My voice was thick with desire. "Like . . . what?"

"I don't know. We'll just have to try."

"I'm not into experimental sex."

"You don't like me, Taki?"

"Of course I do." I was surprised at how sad she sounded and quickly added more reassurance. "This isn't a question of like or dislike. It's a question of mood."

"Really?" A chilling light flashed deep in Makie's eyes. "Then maybe this will help things along. . . ."

She gently exhaled. When her hot breath brushed my ear, I was instantly filled with an indescribable, deep-seated feeling of contentment. Was this a demonic technique? No, it was just a side effect. I was in love with a woman from the *other side*. A woman who, behind her human form, concealed an appearance the nature of which I could not even guess at.

Something other than simple passion and psychological love was arousing me—a more primitive form of desire, along with a feeling of . . . *duty*.

I pushed my left hand deeper inside her. The feeling was slightly alien, but also amazingly soft, warm, and wet. I withdrew, massaging the swollen lips of her vagina before pushing two fingers deep inside her again, giving her clit a soft stroke with my thumb. Makie trembled and threw her head back and let out a moan of pleasure.

"Yes . . . Take me, right here."

"I will. Let's go to the bedroom."

But Makie refused my attempts to remove her from my lap. "We don't need a bed. I want you inside me now. Do me like your animals do it, here on the floor." She whispered into my ear. "Fuck me from behind."

With that, Makie placed her white arms around my neck, dropping us to the floor together.

We kissed for a while longer before I stood and started to undress. As I was taking my shirt off, Makie knelt in front of me and undid my belt. She pulled my pants down and moved my briefs aside, exposing my rock-hard penis. Her unreadable, mysterious expression did not change even when her lovely mouth wrapped around my cock. It was a struggle not to simply give in to the warm moistness of her mouth and skillful attentions of her tongue.

She must have read my thoughts. "Yes, that's it. Come if you want to," Makie said in a breathless voice. I glimpsed her breasts below me, pink with desire, erect nipples and soft curves burning into my brain. Having given me the blow job of my life, Makie turned and waited on all fours.

I gripped her ass with both hands and slid deep inside her. As I thrust in and out of her tight pussy, I stimulated her asshole with one finger. Makie moaned and pushed back toward me. "Yes. Yes. Don't stop."

She was so tight, so hot and wet, I couldn't hold off any longer. I came with a deep shudder. Even as I poured my seed into her, my hand reached for the metal ashtray.

I wasn't even facing the door as the knob dropped away with a popping sound. I was too busy enjoying my orgasm. Feeling Makie's body shudder and her pussy tighten as she came, too, sent me over the edge, and I moaned in ecstasy. My right hand reacted anyway, and the

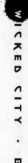

ashtray connected at almost 100 kilometers an hour with the dark shadow that stood in the open doorway.

The missile jammed into his chest. The figure flew backwards, taking the two behind him back into the corridor outside. My Psy Power was back to full strength.

"Taki, fuck me again." Makie was still moving, her slick vagina still rubbing along my length. My cock was almost hard again. "I want you so bad, I want to come again. I'm so close."

It was hard to resist, but we had to take care of business. "Something else has come up."

She thrust back a few more times, her pussy gave another spasm, she moaned again, and then stopped. She slid off my cock.

"I'll help you see to that, then."

The three shadows stood again and stepped into the light. They were typical thugs, dressed in polo shirts and sunglasses, but they weren't human. It was pretty obvious—the ashtray was still buried in the chest of the leader.

Makie stepped forward, ready to fight even though she was still naked.

I took a smoke from the case, lit up, and waited my turn.

Two of the men pulled knives from their shirts and stood ready. They ignored me and went for Makie, one left, one right. They attacked simultaneously. Rather than trying to move aside, Makie simply spun on the spot. The blades, both aimed at her stomach, just slid off her skin. The men staggered to a halt in surprise. I doubted they understood that their failure was a result of the timing of Makie's spin combined with the sweat on her body.

Makie grabbed the collar of each polo shirt and tossed the men into the air. It was like lightning striking from the ground. A sound like eggs breaking erupted above Makie's head. The skulls of the two burly men had been shattered in one strike by a beautiful naked woman.

Rather than a rain of blood and brains, insectlike creatures fell from the bodies. They crawled across Makie's breasts, shoulders, thighs, and buttocks, leaving a sticky trail on her body and wriggling for a while before slowing and then stopping.

The ashtray man stood up and made a quick movement. There was a flash of silver, and I leaned away to avoid it. It continued past me and punched through the steel door. One of the knives was buried up to the hilt in the metal.

Makie had the second knife in her hand. She slammed it against the throat of the remaining attacker and pushed him against the wall.

"Where is Mayart?" she asked. She sounded like a machine.

The man gave a slight shake of his head. "No idea. We were only told to attack you. Don't know anything about him."

"You're telling the truth." Makie glanced in my direction. "It will be dawn soon. We need to . . ."

The man moved his right hand so fast, it was hard to see. He grabbed Makie's hand and took the knife from her

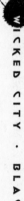

easily. With a manic expression on his face, he made to put his new weapon to use.

But Makie already had a hank of his hair in her hand and she was pulling hard. I wasn't sure which of them made the sharp gasp. With an effortless motion, Makie ripped the man's entire head off. Something inhuman jutted from the torn neck.

It looked like a giant mollusk. It flopped onto the floor and wriggled like a human tongue for a while. But as the head to which it was still attached paled in death, so, too, did its movements die down, eventually ceasing altogether.

"That takes care of that," Makie said, picking the rest of the bugs from her body. "It doesn't look like this place is protected. Let's get out of here. I need a shower first, though."

I said nothing, thinking about where Mayart might be. A noise out in the corridor stopped us both cold. We turned as one to look at the door. Someone was there. Another enemy?

The bizarre presence drew closer, and I sensed that whatever it was, it could easily overpower even our combined PP. I remembered what Chairman had said back in the hospital. Demons had been collecting body parts. Was the result of their experiments outside our door?

The presence stopped just before the open door, still out of sight. Perhaps he was assessing the situation.

We weren't about to wait to find out. Makie and I fired everything we had into the doorway. Presence clashed with presence. The aura our target gave off alone was enough to repel our attack.

Through the thick concrete, I felt our target breaking into a smile. Was this the end?

Without warning, the eldritch presence suddenly scattered. It was there, and then it wasn't—gone without a sound.

Nothing moved. Not even the air stirred . . . until another presence arrived in the corridor. This one was smaller but no less powerful. And very, very familiar.

Makie and I looked at each other. I shook my head. "No . . . it can't be?"

"Good morning, you two." Mayart greeted us in Italian, smooth and fluent in his mother tongue as one would expect. While his greeting was light, there was none of his former carefree self in his smile.

3

UR CAR sped beneath a quickly paling sky toward the site of the signing ceremony in Shinjuku. "So, did you do the nasty?" Mayart asked us. There was no hint of joking in his tone.

"You mean you can't tell just by looking at us?" I said, straight-faced, hands on the wheel. The car had come from the parking lot back at the Crossovers Section. Makie had been given the key by Supervisory Section.

Mayart smiled. "Well, well, you did, then! That's good to hear, excellent, excellent. You'll have to care for the baby, both of you."

"Isn't it a little soon to be offering such advice?" I checked on Makie in the rearview mirror. Perhaps a little embarrassed, she fixed her gaze on something out the window.

Mayart shrugged. "Well, anyway. It's almost dawn. They're going to throw everything they've got at us. I hope you are ready."

I gripped the wheel a little tighter. "As we'll ever be. Perhaps you can share with us where you have been all this time?"

Mayart chuckled. "Somewhere very nice."

Making no more progress on that front, we reached Shinjuku without further incident.

"Oh, there's one more thing," Mayart said. "It isn't going to be me or you they come after now. It will be Makie. Don't drop your guard."

"What?" I whipped my head around to look at Mayart. "Why her?"

I received no reply. A moment later, the famous Shinjuku skyline appeared in front of the car. The ceremony was to be performed on a piece of city-owned land below the expressway that cut through Shinjuku.

"We should just make it," Mayart said, checking his watch. "It's four fifty-five. We have five minutes."

"Plenty of time." I let my irritation show in my voice as we took the wide curve that led to the western underground entrance. Yeah, five minutes was more than enough time for them to take out Mayart. All they had to do was stop him from reaching the ceremony. We were allowed to be three minutes late. That meant they had to hold us up for eight minutes.

But something else was going on here; Mayart had said the demons would be aiming for Makie.

The tension in my chest didn't ease until we blasted up the passageway that led to the site. A combination of Black Guard from both sides had the area around the station completely surrounded. There was no chance of an eldritch space being opened here. No matter how powerful the Militants might be, they didn't have the strength to smash through defenses like these.

Signs of the battles that had taken place in the days leading up to this event were still very much in evidence, however. Stains of both melted demons and human blood appeared along the sides of the road. The tall concrete buildings that surrounded us kept the road practically enclosed, so the Psychic Power released had not totally dissipated. Some of it still lingered on the streets. Coming into contact with it unprepared could cause unconsciousness or sudden dementia. Like during the west exit bus arson incident.

Our car passed the station, and the Kyo-o Plaza Hotel rose up on our left as we continued along. We had just passed it when the earth suddenly rumbled behind us.

The tunnel we had just passed through collapsed, buried under a pile of concrete as though demolished by dynamite.

"Here he comes." Mayart gave an out-of-place laugh. "Finally, my turn."

A black crack appeared in the road at our side, and an avalanche of destruction blocked the road. An instant later, a shadow plummeted from the skies and landed atop the mountain of rubble.

The figure must have jumped from a building—all of which were forty stories tall. That wasn't going to end well.

"This should be right up my alley. I've let you two handle everything until now because you could, but not this time." Mayart opened the door and started to climb out.

"Hold it!" I grabbed Mayart by the arm. "If I let you go out there, we'll have failed in our duty to guard you. It's most important you get to the signing ceremony—"

"You're going to perform the signing," Mayart said quietly.

". . . What?"

"You still don't get it? I haven't been under *your* guard. I was called here from Italy in order to guard you two."

I looked at Makie, shocked. She was obviously surprised as well, but her reaction suggested that she had suspected what Mayart was saying. "I see," was her only reply.

With this new information, all Mayart's capering and seemingly sexually motivated actions took on a new light.

"You saved me in Arakawa?"

"That's right."

"But . . . why? What's this all been about?" I looked at the large approaching figure. The only weapon he carried was a knife, like the guys back in the apartment. It didn't look like he even needed that.

"Let's start with this: A type of mental exchange, or perhaps I should say a strong form of sympathy, has started to flow between the two worlds recently." Mayart shook off my hand and climbed from the car. Of course, I followed him. I still wasn't sure what was going on, but my original orders had been to protect the old man.

Our attacker stopped about five meters in front of us. He wore a black T-shirt and jeans. There was something odd about him, besides his size. He looked . . . irregular. It wasn't his clothing, but the body inside. Halfway up his neck, a *step* jutted from the flesh. His left and right hands were at least ten centimeters different in length. And his entire body leaned to the side—his right leg was shorter than his left.

This was what we had sensed back at the apartment. A monster made from a combination of mismatched body parts into which foul life had been breathed. Our final obstacle. He was certainly responsible for cracking the road, if not taking out the exit behind us, too.

Mayart continued his explanation, apparently not fazed by the gigantic creature before us. "Research from both sides revealed that this link went beyond a simple telepathic exchange. It was also physical sympathy . . . a

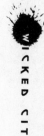

WICKED CITY · BLACK GUARD

phenomenon that extends right down to the genetics of both sides."

". . . I see." I really didn't, but this wasn't quite the time to ask the million questions I had in my mind. I moved away from the car. So did Mayart. Neither of us tried to stop the other. We had left any chance of that behind when we stepped from the car to face our enemy.

"The biggest stumbling block to a real exchange between the two sides has always been the fact that we are genetically incompatible. No matter how much PP a human or demon might have, it just didn't work. But with this newly discovered link, those on both sides have started to appear with *compatible* DNA. Perhaps it is a spiritual representation of the thousands of years of cooperation between us, I don't know. Such compatibility alone is not enough for a child of mixed blood to be produced, however. The hard science was easy. It was finding the appropriate bond between the parents that has been the most difficult to analyze. After years of research, scientists from both sides deduced that the best possible couple to produce a combined-species offspring was you and Makie."

"What the hell!" I wasn't sure if I was yelling at the enemy, who drew even closer, or at Mayart's announcement. He ignored me, either way.

"You two are capable of creating a baby with both human and demonic attributes. A baby that carries with it the possibility of an entirely new breed of being—a whole

new world, if you will. That's why the Militants are so worked up." He waved the thought away. "Enough talk. Here he comes."

For something made from spare parts, the monster moved with amazing speed. With a single leap, he lifted into the air, headed toward the car—and for Makie, still seated in the back.

His legs were extended, ready to kick. Before he reached his target, the attacker was thrown five meters in the opposite direction, landing with a dull thud on the pavement in front of the station. The monster had been thrown by Mayart's PP. His presence was overwhelming. It also explained why I had been unable to gauge his power—at this level, hiding his strength would be as easy for him as breathing.

The creature picked himself up as if he had merely tripped over an uneven section of pavement. He dashed to the car before we could stop him, grabbed the bumper in both hands, and lifted the vehicle into the air without difficulty.

I launched a right body blow into his exposed middle. My fist was infused with as much Psy Power as I could cram into it, and my target moaned. He staggered and dropped the car, which bounced away.

Makie was in danger. My second shot, aimed at his face, was blocked easily. Now it was my turn to be sent flying onto the concrete roadway. The impact shook my whole body.

Mayart joined me with a heavy thud. He sighed and leaned his head back on the pavement. "PP can't damage him. Bloody monster!"

The monster was tearing the doors from the car. I had to help Makie. I struggled to my feet, dizzy.

The monster thrust his hand into the rear seats.

No! Makie!

Before the thought had fully formed in my mind, the monster was thrown into the air. I watched in amazement as he grew, as if someone were pumping air into him. In a few seconds, he was transformed from terrifying monster to overinflated balloon.

He popped.

I looked at Mayart in surprise. We didn't even try to avoid the incoming chunks of flesh as we dashed toward the car—toward Makie.

A white hand extended from the car. Makie's hand. It was the hand that had, with a single blow, dispatched the enemy Mayart and I had been unable to defeat.

Mayart wore a cryptic smile. "Just as I thought. Receiving your seed has transformed her. Indeed, she may already be with child."

And I thought *I* had hit my head. Mayart must have gotten a full concussion. "That can't be. It hasn't been all that long since we did it."

"Black Guard from both sides . . . and powerful, skillful ones at that. This isn't unexpected," Mayart said with a shrug.

I wondered what Makie's father was like. This could bring a whole new meaning to "shotgun wedding."

Mayart's voice brought me out of my reverie. "There was one condition vital to this experiment. According to the Research Section, sex between you two could not be forced. You had to really love each other, had to fully give your hearts and bodies to each other during your bonding. That is the only way to achieve such a genetic transformation as this. That's why I've been messing with you two so much, taking you to all those places and whatnot. And it was exhausting work, I can tell you."

I said nothing, for I was physically unable to speak. A pairing between this world and the demonic one had been achieved, and a baby of both worlds would be born. I had no idea what our baby was going to look like, but it was hard not to feel proud of the achievement. By the time he or she reached our age, the gap between the two worlds might already have vanished. We might be bringing about not just the birth of a child, but also the birth of a new world, one no one had yet experienced.

"Come on, then." Mayart took Makie's hand and helped her out of the car. "This car can't carry us on, but our feet can. We've still got, what, three or four minutes? The ceremony is going to officially recognize the successful coupling of parents from both worlds. Which is you two."

Makie looked at me and smiled. Why was it that women—human or demon—could so easily accept and adapt to circumstances? The smile I gave her in return was wry, but soon it changed into a real smile—a smile for my child, already taking shape inside Makie.

Who knew what the new era would bring? As we started up the mountain of rubble in front of us, I was sure none of us did. But I was willing to wait and find out.

About the Author

Hideyuki Kikuchi is the author of *Demon City Shinjuku, Wicked City,* and *Vampire Hunter D.* He is considered to be the master horror writer of Japan by American fandom, and is often compared to Stephen King.